The Healers

The Healers

Donna Labermeier

The Healers
Copyright © 2011 Donna Labermeier

For more information visit www.myidentifiers.com

Book design by:
Arbor Books, Inc.
www.arborbooks.com
Printed in the United States of America

The Healers
Donna Labermeier

1. Title 2. Author 3. Young Adult Fiction

Library of Congress Control Number: 2011912924
ISBN 13: 978-0-615-51658-5

*I would like to dedicate this work
to my family and friends for their love,
encouragement, and support
throughout this exciting journey.*

Table of Contents

CHAPTER 1

Despair in the Forest

On the day they had decided to kill themselves, Mr. and Mrs. Watanabe woke early and lay in bed not speaking for almost an hour.

Birdsong fluted outside the window of their studio apartment, but it was gradually drowned out by the ugly rumble of the city stirring below. They winced as the illumination grew behind the blinds until it filled the room with a meager light the color of dirty dishwater.

Katsu Watanabe was twenty-five, his wife, Moriko, twenty-two. Come the autumn they would be married for three years. Now, though, that anniversary would never be celebrated. It was the fourth of June, 2004. Today was the date of their *shinjū*, their double suicide. Just like in the infamous Bunraku play by Monzaemon, they would die together in a state of poignant love and make a peaceful ending.

But Moriko didn't feel peaceful. She lay motionless next to Katsu with a knot of dread growing in her stomach. She wanted to say something, to wrench them out of this swan dive, but simply couldn't find the words.

After all the terrible misfortunes that had befallen them, it had been almost a relief to make this pact and end their suffering. But in retrospect that pact had torn a hole in the center of their lives, and silence had come pouring through like a slowly inflating balloon. Moriko could no longer talk to Katsu. He seemed so very far away.

In the days that followed, when they sat in the kitchenette to eat their budget steamed rice and thin miso, Moriko would watch Katsu and know what he was thinking as he stared blankly at the dirty surfaces, the objects they no longer owned, the box of overdue bills on the countertop. He was saying repeatedly to himself, "I have failed." But he couldn't utter the words out loud, so Moriko was never able to throw him a lifeline and tow them both back to shore.

Lying in bed, Moriko realized that she couldn't remember the last time they had laughed together. She was gripped by the conviction that if she could just recall a time when they'd been truly happy, then she could reach her husband. She thought of their wedding day and how giddy she had felt then, but even as she tried to recapture that joy the colors in her memory started to drain away, leaving just monochromatic skeletons. In their turn those silhouettes grew wispy and blew to ashes.

Moriko reached out trembling fingertips to her husband, trying to bridge the chasm between them...but Katsu rocked onto his side, erecting a wall between them. Moriko clenched her fingers into a fist.

There was nothing left to say. Moriko wasn't strong enough to fight this fate.

■ ■ ■ ■ ■

The drive from the Tokyo suburbs to Aokigahara Jukai forest was uneventful. Droning along the Chuo Expressway to Kawaguchiko, Mount Fuji hovered like an alien mother ship on the horizon, impossibly distant and serene and indifferent to all human concerns. A few handfuls of gray drizzle dashed against the windshield, but by the time they reached the parking lot the rain had completely dried away, like tears in a warm summer breeze. Fewer than half of the parking spaces were occupied, and they saw no other drivers, almost as if heralds had run ahead to clear the way so there would be no witnesses to their final walk. They left the keys in the ignition, the doors unlocked, and walked towards the tree line.

Passing over the threshold into Aokigahara Forest was like stepping through the veil into a twilight realm. In fact Moriko felt like they were *already* walking in the spirit world as they moved onto the shadow-drenched pathway between the vast, white-cedar and boxwood trees. It only added to her feelings of inevitability.

The proper translation of Aokigahara Jukai was *sea of green foliage*, but everyone called it the "sea of trees" or just "suicide forest," a primordial sprawl spilling out over seven hundred acres, bedded in volcanic rock spewed up from Mount Fuji somewhere in the mists of time. It was a lopsided, gloomy land of endless slopes and whispering ravines, secret clearings and untamed flora, with a constant taint of death in the air.

The alien quality of the light was what Moriko really couldn't get used to, this perpetual violet shroud here beneath the ominous canopy. It made her feel like she was stumbling in a trance as they trekked along the hikers' trail.

They carried on for about half a mile, past signs directing

backpackers towards the famous lava caves, before other messages began to appear. Sad slogans that clutched at Moriko's heart, placed on the guideposts to try to prevent further suicides: "Please consult the police before you decide to die!" one cried out, while another warning pleaded, "Please reconsider!"

In shame, Moriko averted her eyes and walked on with her gaze firmly planted on the path ahead. This was how she almost collided with Katsu when he stopped dead in his tracks. Moriko held her breath in anticipation. Suddenly her husband plunged off the trail into the shadowy undergrowth like he was diving beneath the surface of a fast-flowing stream: off the track, past the point of no return.

Moriko swallowed. Choosing her footing with care, she dutifully followed. For just a second she thought she heard distant laughter. A child's voice, bell-like and uninhibited, but she dismissed it as her imagination and pushed on into the denser press of trees.

Beyond the trail, Aokigahara lost any semblance of domestication. Tree limbs twisted together like the ghastly arms of wrestling demons; huge, rotten logs loomed while spurs of rust-hued mushrooms exploded out of dark hollows wherever you turned. A mossy, green carpet covered the forest floor, which was strewn with fallen branches, creepers and glittering cobwebs, an open invitation to twist your ankle at every step.

After a short while, with Katsu forging tirelessly ahead, Moriko came upon a bough festooned with scraps of plastic tape fluttering in the breeze. The streamers were grubby with lichen now, but Moriko recalled how hikers wishing to penetrate the hidden heart of the forest would use such pointers to navigate their return. Compasses didn't function properly in Aokigahara due to some unusual magnetic quality of the lava rock—though in this subterranean gloom it was easier to imagine it was the work of malign tree spirits flicking the needles back and forth.

If you lost your way in this shadowy interior, you might never be found. That was why the hikers brought their tape, but it was also why people such as she and Katsu were drawn to Aokigahara. When she had been trying to reconcile her heart with their plan, Moriko had read Tsurumi's notorious cult book on suicide, in which he described the sea of trees as "the perfect place to die." But standing here Moriko only felt a helpless sense of growing foreboding. The prospect of passing away in such an empty, brooding place seemed quite horrible. She found that she was not resigned to this fate at all.

Suddenly there was a rustle in the branches, and Moriko whipped around to catch the fleeting impression of motion. Once more she thought she heard a child's laughter.

"K-katsu?" Moriko called out. "I think someone might be following us…"

But her husband had broken out into an open glade with a brackish stream, and did not answer. Moriko reluctantly joined him in the center of the clearing.

"Here," he whispered. Katsu faltered for a breath or two, his expression more perplexed than upset, like he was trying to work out a complicated puzzle. "Here is where we shall rest."

Moriko knew he meant that they would never leave this place. Katsu avoided her gaze as he removed two small bottles from his backpack. Moriko flinched. She didn't know exactly what they contained—Katsu had taken upon himself the most distasteful details of their (*his*) plan—but she knew that it would be swift, and the first taste would be very bitter. They would pull faces at that sour flavor, blink away the tears, then lie down together on the bed of springy moss-covered ground and fall asleep.

Only Katsu was fretting. He couldn't decide which was *the* perfect place for their final rest and danced agitatedly from spot to spot, almost hysterical with indecision. Moriko was torn. While she found it heartbreaking to see Katsu reduced to this state, every moment he dithered held out the hope that he might change his mind. Moriko bowed as she bit her hand in silent anguish. When she straightened she found that a young girl had appeared in front of her!

The girl was aged about eight or nine and dressed in a blue summer dress. She wore her straight, glossy hair in neat braids and was beaming from ear to ear with the most genuine, most infectious smile Moriko had ever seen.

"Hello, I'm Koemi," said the girl. "Who are you?"

In spite of herself, Moriko couldn't help but smile at the girl's warmth.

"I—I'm Moriko," she stammered.

"You don't have to be sad, Moriko. Everything's going to be all right."

Moriko risked a glance over her shoulder at Katsu, who was so agitated he hadn't even noticed there was someone else present. Perhaps Koemi was just a ghost conjured by Moriko's disordered mind. But then Koemi reached out and touched Moriko's cheek with a cool, soft palm. She was quite real. Her touch granted Moriko the overwhelming sensation of wholeness and serenity she had been seeking.

"*Ohayo*, Katsu!" the girl called out to Moriko's distraught husband, a joyous, informal greeting as if he were an old family friend. Katsu spun around and stared open-mouthed.

"Who are you? How do you know my name?" he gasped.

"I heard Moriko call you it, silly! Come on, let's play a game!" Koemi happily announced and dodged into the undergrowth.

"We have to catch her!" Katsu babbled, his resolve openly crumbling. Something in Moriko's chest leapt with hope. "No one must know...where we are. It'll spoil our...rest. Spoil everything!"

Katsu began to scour the bushes for Koemi. Moriko joined in, trembling with emotion. Every time they were about to catch the girl she would slip past them like an eel through the fingers of a clumsy fisherman. Koemi teased Moriko and Katsu with giggles and glimpses, always one lunge out of reach behind the next bush or tree trunk. Soon Moriko found herself lightheaded and reeling, bursting out laughing. By contrast Katsu was hard-faced, but as his cheeks grew redder and his breath shorter, even he started to grin.

Moriko leaned against a nearby tree, chest heaving. Katsu made a final leap at Koemi but fell short and collapsed in a heap on the forest floor, overcome. Koemi appeared in front of him, smiling down with an expression of total acceptance. Katsu blinked at her in wonderment. The girl beckoned to Moriko. Koemi took her hand and offered her other palm to Katsu. He stared at the extended hand but withheld his grasp.

"What's your happiest memory?" Koemi asked.

"I—I can't remember..." Katsu whispered hoarsely after an agonizing pause.

"I do!" Moriko cried. "Our wedding day, do you remember, Katsu? The *san-san-kudo* ceremony was so old-fashioned, and I couldn't stop getting the giggles. Then you were hilarious afterwards, posing for all the children in your robes, dancing like a clown!"

For such a long time silence had choked Moriko, but now words came tumbling out of her. "And all the colors—the cherry blossoms in spring! Those colors are still inside of us, Katsu, I know it. We were so happy just a short time ago!"

A smile crept gingerly across Katsu's face, gradually unravelling the knots that had bitten into his brows.

"I…remember laughing," he finally admitted.

"Laughter isn't just what happens when you hear a funny joke," said Koemi with a giggle. "It rescues you on days as dark as this! It makes the light inside of you grow brighter and brighter until the darkness can't touch you. Laughter chases your fears away, tosses them out into space far, far away. Whatever terrible things happen in your life you must laugh at yourselves. Say to yourself, 'All is well. I am joyous and happy and free.' The Universe will hear you. Like a mirror, it will reflect back that joy upon you! Laughter can save you from despair, and it's contagious—I can pass it on to you."

Koemi laughed then, and Katsu did, too, startling Moriko, a full-throated bark of joy like she hadn't heard him utter in months and months. "Then you can pass it back to me," Koemi finished, with a meaningful look to Moriko, who joined in with the mirth.

As their voices rose up towards the tops of the trees, Moriko was aware of a warm sensation passing through her whole body. It was as though Koemi were acting as a conduit for an *energy* source that was fountaining out of the natural world, allowing their inner happiness to grow. Moriko had been wrong to think of this place as painfully morbid… It was the place that would save them!

Moriko knew then that all would be well. She and Katsu would return home, and whatever setbacks might assail them, the silence of despair would never drown them again. Their lives—like this clearing—would echo with joy for many decades to come, embracing the fun and playful adventure of unexpected things happening along the way.

■ ■ ■ ■ ■

Koemi stood in the center of the glade and watched Moriko and Katsu head back towards the hikers' trail. When they were just within the limit of visibility, she raised her palm to wave but wasn't sure if they saw her.

Before they left, Moriko had taken Koemi's hand and pressed it to her breast, whispering that she was their angel of mercy. Koemi smiled to herself. She had managed to draw two more souls back from the brink. It was only one couple, granted, but in the months since she had discovered her ability to channel this sustaining energy of nature through her laughter, Koemi had saved as many lost souls as she could find in Aokigahara Jukai. She was *sure* she was making a difference.

Still, though, she was troubled. Just now, when she had been coaxing the couple back to the light, she had detected something that the Watanabes had not. It was something only someone long-attuned to the moods of the forest would have picked up on. Koemi had heard another voice behind their laughter, a dark, sarcastic snickering that had echoed their pure merriment.

Koemi had roamed this forest since she was a toddler, first with her family, then on her own. She felt a profound sadness for those souls driven to take their own lives, but she had never once felt fear in this place. Until now. She imagined that cold, unblinking eyes were even now watching her from the gloom...

Koemi knew she could not linger. Today was her birthday and she needed to get back before her mother began to worry. Maybe this foreboding was just her imagination after all. With one last edgy glance around the clearing, Koemi shivered, then set off for home.

Behind her, *something* chuckled in the dark hollows of the sea of trees...

CHAPTER 2

I Can Fly!

Every night, in her dreams, Harata flew.

At first she would be doing something utterly mundane. Sometimes she dreamt of lying on her bedroll in her family's cramped but colorful house. On other occasions, she'd be walking through the crowds of Lahore's Walled City, or sitting on Food Street in Gawalmandi at night, nibbling delicious *chapli* kebabs off skewers in the shadow of the centuries-old buildings. *Then* she would feel a gentle tug.

It wasn't like someone had touched her shoulder; it was a sensation she experienced throughout her whole body. It was a delightful tingling that seemed to be saying, "This is natural, this is right, if you follow this pull you will be so free!"

In her dreams Harata immediately surrendered to the tug. She slipped free of her body like she was wriggling out of a silk sleeping bag. As her point of view levitated upwards she was able to look down upon the pretty, fierce-faced girl she occasionally glimpsed in the mirror as she rushed out to play in the streets. (Harata was an incorrigible tomboy, and checking her appearance was NEVER her most pressing concern!)

Then Harata hurtled up above the streets, her awareness whirling and spinning uncontrollably. It was always the same. She would pull herself out of her body, then instantly lose control. Her bodiless spirit had no weight and was completely invisible. It was impossible to get your bearings if you couldn't see or feel your hands or feet, or _any_ of your extremities—because you didn't have any!

These dreams had persisted for well over a month now. Slowly Harata was learning to tame the phenomenon. So now she only suffered a moment's disorientation before being able to control her hovering spirit. She expended a few seconds laughing at all the little stick people trapped in the noisy, hot crowds below, then launched herself up over the rooftops with a joyous shriek that only she could hear.

Harata was filled with a giddy joy at this wonderful freedom. The sensation of limitless acceleration was incredible as she swept across her city. She marvelled at the tangled maze that composed the Inner City, the dense beating heart of Lahore, and her home, known also as Andheron Shehr to many. She enjoyed how the streets were thronged with bodies in rainbow-bright fabrics, how the pedestrians fearlessly competed for space with push-bikes and Qingqi auto-rickshaws, minivans and smart air-conditioned buses from the Saami Daewoo service all shoving together in an endless, pulsing, lively scrum.

Harata delighted at the street stalls selling sandals, silk shawls, fruit of every kind, radios, garlands of onion and garlic. There were such sprawling, vibrant markets down there, like Anarkali on the side of Punjab University Old Campus, reputedly the oldest bazaar in South Asia. Anarkali was named after a legendary slave girl who'd been buried alive by the Mughal emperor Akbar for falling in love with Prince Jahangir. Harata thought that if *she* were ever buried alive, she would be able to subsist for years on dreams of freedom such as these.

In her sleep, Harata's senses were dulled by some quirk of dream logic, but still she was able to detect the gorgeous stew of scents and sounds that drifted up from below: spices, burning incense, the mingled fragrance of a thousand ravishing dishes; the *dholak* drum percussion, the sitar melodies and harmonium solos that played counterpoint to the car horns and the sea of happy, angry, hopeful voices.

Seeing the metropolis spread out like this she could easily recognize the influence of the great powers who had ruled the city during its four-thousand-year history: the Mughal and Sikh legacy in the facades of Lahore Fort, Badshahi Mosque and Gurdwara; the colonial-gothic buildings from the British Raj lining the Mall Road, while out in the Gulberg suburbs were the palatial mansions and trendy shopping districts of modern Pakistan. Above the city, kites appeared as silhouetted darts, swooping and fluttering while the Lahore citizenry practiced for the world-famous Basant Hindu festival. It made Harata feel very proud.

In her dreams, Harata could fly with far more accuracy than any kite, however, and so she dived down, down, down until she was skimming mere inches above the busy pavements, zipping between people's legs, dodging around stray dogs and strutting cats. All because it was a thrill that a poor girl from the Walled City could never experience in her waking hours.

It was for this same reason that—as her control over the dream grew—Harata started to use her flights to peek into other people's lives. She was a naturally inquisitive soul—or, as her father and four brothers would have it, plain nosy—so this interest was a natural development.

She followed a crotchety old fish seller, Nasir Zulfiqar Hussain, when he slipped away from his shop at three o'clock, and discovered that he went down to the bank of the canal, where he stared across the water with tears in his eyes and a crumpled photo of a woman in Western dress in his lap. She watched the screaming, fighting Masood family at their evening meal and saw that they continued to scream and fight even while shovelling food into their mouths! She chased teenage pickpockets through the crowds at Lahore airport and gasped at the watercolors stern Mr. Lal painted in his apartment at night but would never allow another soul to see. Finally, she rolled her nonexistent eyes at the outrageous lies Fareed Khan told his wife when he'd swaggered home from an evening spent in the park with one of his many mistresses.

Harata was devout (mostly), she prayed (*quite* often), but unlike other members of her family she wasn't superstitious. She didn't believe that these dreams contained any mystical portent but couldn't explain why they kept recurring every night! Despite her rough-and-tumble nature, Harata was a dedicated student and a voracious reader. She had always applied herself to her schoolwork with an intense dedication, especially after she discovered how lucky she was to be receiving an education. In Pakistan so many girls weren't allowed to attend schools, either due to poverty or inflexible tradition.

Harata learned from her gentlest brother, Syed, that the only reason she'd been allowed to attend school was a deathbed promise their mother had wrung out of Papa Kedar while she lay mortally injured in the hospital following a dreadful traffic accident near the Kashmiri gate. Kedar was a stern, pious, difficult man, but he always kept his word. So, in memory of their poor lost mother, Harata went to school. She learned her letters, excelled in Urdu and Punjabi classes, and even spoke English like a native (or, at least, that was what she shouted at the tourists she enjoyed pestering in Al Falah Square).

It was actually in a magazine that Harata found an explanation for her nighttime excursions. The dog-eared journal had been picked up by her teacher, Muhammad Saleem Rana, on his last holiday to England, and he passed it on to some of his most promising students. In the magazine she found an article on lucid dreaming, a state in which dreamers actually became aware that they were dreaming *while* they were still asleep. Following that revelation they were actually able to control their dreams! Harata was convinced this was the answer. It would explain how vivid her dream flight felt and how much control she had over events. After this discovery, Harata counted herself as a truly blessed girl, since lucid dreaming was a rare skill indeed.

On the night of the fourth of June, 2004, Harata dreamt that she was in the Ichhra Bazaar, playing a game of tag with her friends, Salima and Zinah. However, when the lucid dreaming *tug* came, that was when the real excitement began. That night, she wanted to experiment with something other than flying...

Since she'd discovered lucid dreaming, Harata had come up with a number of ways to test the limits of her control over the dream world. She was particularly intrigued by the ability of her spirit body to pass like a ghost through any surface. When she was little, Harata had watched a fuzzy VHS copy of an American film called *Ghost*, in which disembodied spirits could pass straight through people, and this got her thinking. Even if it was only a dream she wanted to see if her subconscious would let her slide through another living body and what that would feel like.

Harata still wasn't bold enough to fly straight through a person. Even if it wasn't real, it somehow still felt like a violation. Instead, she sped down a narrow alleyway after a pack of stray dogs. She rocketed towards a small, black terrier that was bringing up the rear. She flew so close she could actually make out individual dirt flecks matted in the dog's hair. She dived forward.

Harata didn't go *through* the dog, as she had expected—she was somehow *inside* the animal's thoughts! She was being carried along with the jouncing, scampering motion of his gait, and she could feel his little paws as *her* hands and *her* feet striking the pavement! Her vantage was low to the ground, chesting excitedly through drifts of trash, and her (his?) nostrils were filled with an overpowering blend of intoxicating scents: rotten mango and spoiled steak, charcoal, perfume, scorched rubber... It was overwhelming. The dream flight above the city had been exhilarating, but *this*—experiencing the world through the dog's senses—was so intense it was almost unbearable.

Harata yearned to run faster. She wanted to chase and leap, desperately shoving to get ahead of her fellows as they erupted out of the mouth of the alley in a skidding, biting mass of hair and teeth and—

Suddenly she was being shaken awake. A furious face loomed overhead like a moon crashing down upon her. For a moment Harata was truly afraid, and gasped out loud...only to realize that the crashing moon face was just her sulky older brother, Tahir.

"Where are they? What did you do with them, you little sneak?" he shouted as he shook her like a bundle of sticks.

Harata didn't have the faintest clue what Tahir was going on about, and told him so in no uncertain terms. Tahir pinched her arms tighter, causing Harata to lash out with her long legs. Tahir grunted like a hog before leaping out of range. He glared down at her, his breath coming and going in tight, hot little gusts.

"What did you do with my sunglasses, you street rat?" Tahir hissed, his neck twisted against the low-sloping ceiling.

Their whole family lived crammed together in a crumbling, third-story townhouse in the center of the Old City. Tahir had to share a room with their three other brothers. Papa Kedar claimed the only private space, which could serve both as a sleeping area and an office. As the only female, Harata had been granted the precious gift of her own bedroom. It was little more than a cramped closet, but it was the most wonderful place in the world for Harata—her cherished sanctuary. That Tahir had taken to storming in there whenever he pleased was an impertinence that made her blood boil.

"I didn't move your glasses, donkeyhead!" Harata raged. "You'll have just put them down somewhere and forgotten about it again!"

"You've broken them and tried to cover it up!" Tahir bellowed. "You're always ruining things for the rest of us with your selfish games!"

This was too much, thought Harata, and on her birthday as well. Of course, they were Muslims and didn't celebrate birth as people did in the West. After all, what was the logic in celebrating that your life had *decreased* by one more year? (Harata, though, considered herself something of an expert on American culture and did sometimes regret that she didn't get a cake with candles on top.) Even so, it wasn't fair for Tahir to take his ill temper out on her. She'd done all her chores, washed their clothes and prepared chapatis for them to eat that evening. So she took half an hour to lie down. So what? What did Tahir do all day?

Indignation coursed through Harata. It was a heat rising up from her chest, blazing along her throat, threatening to explode...*and that was when she felt the invisible tug!*

In total disbelief, Harata surrendered to the ghostly pull, more out of shock than intent. Suddenly, she was flying exactly as she did in her dreams. Her spirit body instantly flashed off through the nearest wall, whistling over Syed's head in the next room. Then her awareness was drawn along the hallway like a breeze, arcing around corners until it finally zipped into Kedar's room. There her sight focused on something Harata could barely believe. Before she could confirm her vision, she was snapped back into her body like someone had pinged a length of elastic.

Before she knew what she was doing, Harata spat into Tahir's face. "Your sunglasses are under Papa's reading chair, you big oaf!"

Tahir looked shocked for a moment, then his expression clenched back into fury. He dragged Harata kicking and screaming out of the room.

The appalling din they made drew loud protests from all over the house, but Tahir didn't care. He towed Harata grimly on towards his destination, though she noisily fought him every step of the way. They arrived in Kedar's den, where—oblivious to how much trouble they would be in if Papa caught them—they both looked down...and saw Tahir's knockoff Ray-Bans sitting abandoned underneath the threadbare reading chair. There was a long pause.

"You did take them," Tahir finally growled. "You—you must have hidden them to make me angry."

He didn't sound especially convinced, though. Tahir snatched up the sunglasses and stalked away without a word of apology.

Harata barely noticed. She was just staring fixedly at the dusty spot on the floor where she'd seen the missing sunglasses mere moments before.

Harata wasn't a lucid dreamer. Her flying wasn't just a dream.

Harata could project her mind out of her body *while she was still awake...*

CHAPTER 3

Colors
of the Soul

While walking with her mom along Ninth Avenue towards Saint Rafael's Midtown Hospital, Eleanor Henning wasn't surprised to see a German Shepherd mix with a glowing, blue halo.

The dog was tied up outside a minimart, and while her mom, Rachel, dipped inside the store for "emergency supplies", Eleanor hunkered down to pet the animal. She wasn't worried that he would bite her, as she knew that blue was a good color—loyal, calm, peaceful. The mutt endorsed her intuition by panting happily and thwacking his huge tail against an aluminium NY Lottery sign that reverberated like a struck gong.

"Hey, boy," Eleanor whispered. "You and me left out on the street, eh?"

She was still scratching her new friend when Rachel emerged from the shop, a flurry of hands and elbows, stowing her purse while trying to unwrap her emergency supplies at the same time. She lit one of them, then blew away the first puff of smoke with a heartfelt moan. Eleanor watched her mother sadly. The older woman caught her daughter's expression and winced.

"Don't look at me like that, Ellie. Not today."

Eleanor bit her lip. "Sorry, Mom." Eleanor always tried her best not to be resentful, but it was difficult sometimes when her mother seemed totally wrapped up in her own problems. Once again Eleanor felt liked she'd been forgotten in the perpetual headlong plunge that was her mother's life.

The color that illuminated her mother was a rich, swirling magenta, edged with dabs of aquamarine. Eleanor sensed somehow that these hues spoke of her mom's creativity and free spirit, but also showed how vulnerable she could be. Normally it made Eleanor smile to see how Rachel's colors complemented the green scrubs she wore under her denim jacket, but today a swarm of arid tones had begun to invade her corona, splintering its purity with gray, threadlike fissures. Eleanor hated those grays. Gray was the shade of disaster when it came to her mother's moods.

"I'll quit again this summer, I promise," Rachel babbled defensively. "But not today, NOT on the first day of your school break, NOT when all our plans have been blasted to bits by You Know Who!"

Eleanor didn't answer. She said goodbye to the German Shepherd, which—seeming to sense the shifting mood—had began to whine uneasily.

Eleanor joined her mom obediently and they hurried on along the sidewalk, heading towards Hell's Kitchen past high, brick tenements.

"This is all your dad's fault," Rachel told her daughter as they sped on. "We had a deal, and he *promised* you. Start of summer vacation, you and him on the nature trail, tour of the great parks, but oh no, the day before, *the very day before,* he pulls a stunt like this, when it's too late to make any other arrangements…"

While they tramped along Eleanor glumly watched the gray cracks mottling her mother's corona like an infection. Now they were joined by smears of muddy brown, which were the ultimate warning color.

In truth, Eleanor wasn't too disheartened that Dad had cancelled their trip. Somehow she'd sensed it was coming and had been braced for the letdown. She'd been looking forward to spending time with her mom instead, even if that meant accompanying her to work. She loved being with Rachel when she was happy. Happy Mom was AWESOME, full of games and jokes and weird facts and endless mad schemes. Angry, miserable, gray-cracks Mom was the worst, though, and to Eleanor's dismay that was who it seemed she'd be spending her vacation with… It was the pits.

Eleanor had to actively pin her attention on a person to snap their colors into full clarity. Then their auras would become almost painfully crisp. The rancid, gray veins within her mother's halo popped out at Eleanor as she stared. It almost felt like she could reach out and tweak the gray like the strands of silvery hair Rachel plucked off of her own head with a shriek every few days. Eleanor longed to stretch out a palm to those ugly, throbbing filaments…

But that was a childish idea, and Eleanor was not a little girl anymore. She was nine—almost a grownup, really. She snatched her fingers back as Rachel caught the gesture and flashed a disapproving glance. Angry Mom was here to stay.

"Maybe he just loves his new family more," Eleanor let slip before she really knew what she was saying. Rachel jerked to a halt, face crumpling.

"That's NOT true. Your father loves you as much as ANYONE in the world... And even it were true—which it isn't—I've got more than enough love for both of us."

The gray cracks instantly retreated from Rachel's halo. Eleanor grinned an unselfconscious smile, as her mother impulsively hugged her too hard right there on the street.

Eleanor was embarrassed, and her sides hurt because the embrace was so tight, but it still felt great all the same.

■ ■ ■ ■ ■

On the steps to Saint Rafael's, they paused for Rachel to grind out her (latest) cigarette and freshen up her lipstick. Eleanor leaned back to peer up at the sheer brownstone cliff of the hospital above and its thorny crown of towers, turrets and looming cross gables.

Looking at the hospital always gave Eleanor a thrill. Here they helped people. Every day in Saint Rafael's they helped people. Even though she was young, Eleanor knew that helping people was what she was going to do, just like her mom. The problem was, though, that Eleanor was TERRIBLE at all her science classes! There didn't seem to be any realistic chance that she could become a doctor or a nurse, so she would just have to find her own way to help people.

"*Homo sum: humani nil a me alienum puto,*" Eleanor recited under her breath, frowning as she practiced the unfamiliar syllables Rachel had so painstakingly taught her—the hospital motto.

"I am a human being: I regard nothing of human concern as foreign to my interests."

■ ■ ■ ■ ■

The corridors in Saint Rafael's were filled with dazzling reflections and floors that made Eleanor's shoes squeak. The pediatrics ward was decorated in a welcoming shade of sunflower yellow. There were fresh flowers in a vase, lots of wall paintings with child-friendly themes, and, at the nurses' desk, a gallery of kids' sketches pinned up on the cork message boards.

Rachel conferred with a couple of the nurses—a large, friendly-looking African-American lady and a sleepy-eyed young man with a tiny goatee—then dragged a wheeled, comfy chair from a nearby office for Eleanor to camp out on.

"I'll come and check on you every half hour, but one of the other nurses or orderlies will keep an eye on you whenever I'm not around." She pointed to the black woman and the young, male nurse. "That's Ina and that's Billy." Ina and Billy waved.

Eleanor's mother gnawed her lip, her brow creased like used wrapping paper. Eleanor might only have been nine, but she knew how difficult it had been for Rachel since Dad had left. By nature, Eleanor was a quiet, introspective girl and found exaggerated displays of emotion very difficult, but she knew it was up to her to help paper over the cracks, so she grinned as warmly as she could and gently squeezed her mother's arm.

"It'll all be okay, Mom. I'll sit here and draw the people passing by—it'll be fun!"

Her mother's face relaxed in gratitude. "I know we said we'd wait for your party…but why don't you open one of your presents now?"

Amazed, Eleanor took the clumsily but brightly wrapped present Rachel proffered. She carefully slit the paper…to reveal a gleaming set of professional artists' pastels!

Eleanor marvelled at the colors and the quality of the gift. It was exactly the brand she'd been looking at in the little art-supplies shop in Greenwich Village. Her mother had remembered! Maybe this *could* be a great birthday after all. Immediately after this flare of hope, however, Eleanor caught a glimpse of the gray snakes in the colors surrounding her mother as she rushed away.

Eleanor sighed. She took out her sketch pad, clicked open her beautiful birthday pastels, then searched around for someone interesting to draw.

■ ■ ■ ■ ■

Because she was so talented—winner of more art competitions than any other student in the history of their school!—Eleanor's art teacher, Miss Pasky, had repeatedly tried to get her to branch out and try other subjects: landscapes, abstract expressionism, still life. It was all to no avail. There was only one theme that interested Eleanor, to the point where she often only drew the surrounding world as a shadowy background blur. Eleanor drew portraits, and that was it.

So, sitting by herself and drawing all morning was a bit of an unexpected treat for Ellie. She was aware of Ina and Billy keeping a close eye on her, but other than that she was pretty much left alone, which was ideal. The nurses' station provided an excellent vantage point. It let her indulge herself in her favorite pastime: people watching. For such a solitary girl, Eleanor had always been fascinated by the idiosyncrasies of everyone dashing around her.

During that morning it plucked at her heart how many faces looked sad, but she was surprised that so many people also appeared hopeful or expectant, or wept with tears of joy, not grief. Eleanor smiled as she concentrated on her sketches. She drew a rambunctious toddler, his face crinkled with laughter, and surrounded him with a shimmering nimbus of yellow. She focused on a quiet elderly couple walking arm in arm, their hues of softly rippling indigo so similar she instinctively drew one matching veil around them. When a senior doctor arrived and barked stern instructions to the nurses, Eleanor sketched him out with a few angry black slashes and haloed his body in flames of swarming scarlet. Later, when the corridor grew quiet, she drew a simple portrait of nurse Ina's face lit by the highlights of her wise, electric-blue glow.

Eleanor didn't really understand why adults made such a fuss about her artwork. Sure, when compared to the drawings of other kids they looked far more realistic, but when she picked up her pencils it never felt like she was really *trying* very hard. For Miss Pasky art seemed to be all about doggedly learning a laundry list of technical, machinelike lessons—how to render perspective or volume correctly, or the trick to shading perfect shadows. For Eleanor drawing was the most relaxing sensation she knew. It was like the images were flowing in through her eyes, and she was redirecting them, like a bright energy, back out onto the sketch pad. It was probably why she totally lost herself in her drawings. Her fingertips skated over the paper, blending apricots and oranges and vermillion and—

"Why do all the people in your pictures look funny?" someone asked.

Eleanor glanced up in surprise. She hadn't realized how completely wrapped up she'd been. The clock on the wall already read eleven forty. The boy standing over her was about twelve and wearing a crimson flannel gown that he seemed rather proud of. He was constantly fiddling with his cuffs and collars to align them just so. It made him look a little fidgety, but he had a wide, open, freckly face that Eleanor instantly liked.

"Don't you like my drawings?" she tossed back, ignoring the boy's question. It was one that people asked a lot, and there wasn't an easy answer.

The boy frowned. The soft glow that surrounded him was predominantly yellow and turquoise—colors she knew, from experience, represented happiness. Stirring underneath, however, were the ugly patterns that Eleanor had come to recognize as symptoms of sickness. She'd watched how these unsightly colors would shift in patients over time as their conditions progressed.

There were menacing flecks of white in the boy's corona, coiling and looping around each other. Individual spots would sometimes nudge together to form an unexpected fatty lump. In Eleanor's experience, if too many of the white invaders clumped together and obscured the aura's natural color, then their medical prognosis would quickly become dire.

"No, the pictures are good. Really, *really* good," the boy backtracked. "It's just that people don't look like that. They don't have all those." He struggled to conjure up a fitting description. "People don't have those swooshy-wooshy colors dancing around them!" His palms weaved excitably in the air like goldfish at feeding time.

Normally Eleanor would make up a story about how the auras were an important *artistic statement,* which was one of the few useful phrases she'd ever gotten out of Miss Pasky's art books! But something in the boy's face made her want to be honest with him.

"People look like that to *me*," she replied quietly.

The boy stared at her intently for a long while. "You're a bit weird," he finally observed, but in an approving tone. "You wanna come play with me and my friends?"

Eleanor closed up her pastel tin, nodding enthusiastically.

"Great!" The boy grinned. He had a gap between his front teeth so wide it looked like someone had used his incisors as a pen holder. "I'm Cody," he announced. Eleanor offered her palm very politely, like Rachel had taught her, but Cody pumped it up and down like he was trying to draw water from a stubborn well.

Eleanor winced, her jaw jiggering in time with her flailing wrist. "Ellie, you can call me Ellie. Can I have my hand back now, please?"

"Oh, sorry, sorry. I'm so clumsy," replied Cody. He stepped back only to knock a stack of files onto the floor with a papery crash. He shot her a rueful look as he gathered up the spilt pages, then shrugged with a helpless laugh.

"Let's go find the others."

■ ■ ■ ■ ■

Cody's friends had completely taken over a full table in the bustling cafeteria. By the time Eleanor and Cody arrived its top was covered in plastic cups, foil and used plates, condiments, books, sweaters, bags. The kids—two boys and two girls, all between the ages of ten and thirteen—looked eagerly at the newcomers. Eleanor was the youngest person there and looked it, which made her instantly feel out of place.

Cody only made her nervousness worse by proudly announcing, "This is Eleanor, but you HAVE to call her Ellie!"—like he'd discovered her on a jungle expedition and was now posing for photographs in a pith helmet, a musket over one shoulder.

"Hi, ELL-ieee!" all the kids chorused in a sing-song tone, then gazed expectantly at Eleanor, patiently waiting for a reply. Feeling like an exotic animal being displayed behind glass, Eleanor wilted under those curious but relentless stares. In truth Eleanor was a very timid girl, and often, in spite of the things she'd had to deal with in her young life, she felt much less grown up than she appeared to be. Right now she wanted her beloved stuffed toy giraffe, Stanley, to hug.

"Y-you d-don't have to call me Ellie," she stammered.

"Be nice to Ellie because it's her birthday," Cody chided the others, even though he was the one who was digging her ever deeper into a hole! Eleanor shot him a horrified look. She hadn't wanted anyone to know about her birthday. How did he know?

"The nurses told me," Cody confessed in a whispered aside. "They said we should look after you, since you were going to be here on your own for the day. Don't be mad, Ellie, we'll have LOADS of fun."

"Happy birthday, ELL-ieee!" the others sang, laughing.

Ellie thanked everyone, then hid behind her bangs as best as she could. To her delight, Cody and his friends didn't take the slightest bit of notice of her awkwardness and instantly welcomed her into their group. They basically turned lunch-time into an impromptu birthday party. There was (out of tune) singing, there was cake, there were smiles. Eleanor couldn't have asked for a better celebration and ended up grinning so hard her cheeks hurt.

Cody introduced each of his friends as extravagantly as he'd presented Eleanor to the group, with wild boasts and even wilder arm gestures. There was Frank, the oldest and largest, who had huge, green eyes and fat cheeks and, according to Cody, had almost died on the operating table THREE TIMES! Frank was laid back, funny and always shooting out wise-cracks, often at the expense of his great rival, Spencer, a tiny, speedy, motor-mouthed African-American kid obsessed with wrestling and drag racing. Queen of the group was Tammy—delicate, perfect, blonde, but possessing so many nerdy facts about almost any subject you could think of (computers, snakes, chocolate chip cookies) that the others had dubbed her the Human Encyclopedia. Last came Chinese-American Lisa—Tammy's best friend—the rock of the whole group: down to earth, clever, quiet when she needed to be but tough and loud when someone had to be defended. Lisa was someone Eleanor implicitly knew she could trust with her life.

While Frank and Spencer had some kind of war with sugar packets and Cody was trying to impress the girls with a story about a pet eel, Eleanor sat to one side and quietly contemplated her new friends. It was sad to think that the reason she'd met them in the first place was that they were all ill; however, Cody, Frank, Spencer, Tammy and Lisa never once complained or felt sorry for themselves. Eleanor's life hadn't always been easy, it was true, but these kids had faced the darkest of circumstances. And they were still fighting. It made Eleanor feel proud that they'd accepted her into their little group.

"Ellie's a totally amazing artist!" proclaimed Cody, who seemed to be on a one-man mission to drive her into total humiliation. He started passing Eleanor's drawings around the table. The sketchpad pages produced an eruption of coos and amazed gasps, which caused Eleanor to lower her gaze, embarrassed that she was the center of attention yet again. Secretly, she was happy they all liked her art, but this revelation, of course, led to the inevitable questions...

"Why have they got all those funny colors on them?" Tammy asked.

Eleanor had confessed to Cody the truth about her unusual vision because she'd been struck with an instinctive feeling about the warmth of his personality. She just *knew* Cody would understand. However, put on the spot like this, Eleanor felt her cheeks grow hot; she was abruptly terrified that people would think she was some sort of freak. So much of life at school was about fitting in, not standing out from the crowd, and the last thing she wanted to do was to spook these new friends.

"It's a, a fun way to... Well, it's an artistic choice—" she began, but the words were barely out of her lips before Cody abruptly cut her off.

He declared knowledgeably: "That's how she sees people! Eleanor's special!"

"Do you have something wrong with your eyes?" asked Lisa in a sensitive tone. "I can't see so well because of my diabetes, and sometimes I don't even recognize my friends if they walk by me on the street!"

Eleanor's mouth had gone dry, but she told herself to tough

it out. Mere moments ago she'd just been thinking how special her new friends were. Deep down, she *wanted* to tell everyone about her gift, the amazing colors she saw and what they all meant!

"No, my eyes are okay... I just see the colors that surround people. Colors that *our* bodies generate. All of us, animals too—everything living. Our...auras, that's what they're called... I read about them on the Internet. The colors mean different things, what your personality is like, or..."

Eleanor bit her lip. She'd been about to blurt out how the colors also showed how healthy you were, before realizing that it might be an insensitive thing to say in front of her friends. "The colors... It's like they talk to me... But I don't think you have to be special to see them! In fact, I'm sure anyone could do it if they just knew how!"

A hush fell over the table as her words sunk in. Eleanor held her breath, fists clenched under the table. No one looked at anybody else. They were consumed by contemplation. Finally, a slow smile spread across Spencer's face.

"I want to try that," he announced. "That's sounds cooooooooooooooooool!"

The other kids eagerly joined in, so soon Eleanor obediently began trying to teach them. "First try emptying your brain of all thoughts," she said.

"That won't take long for Spence," Frank whispered, which made everybody snicker. Then the learning began.

■ ■ ■ ■ ■

Ironically, given her partial sight, Lisa proved the best at the game. More often than not she identified the same hues as Eleanor, though far less crisply or reliably. Still, it was an excellent start. The others weren't so skilled, though they certainly enjoyed themselves, peering through squashed-up eyes, cocking their heads at weird angles to pull outrageous faces, dissolving into helpless hysterics.

"No fair! I can't see anything!" wailed Frank. "The only colors I'm getting are in black and white—I'm like my grandpa's television!"

Everyone laughed uproariously at that. However their hilarity was immediately curtailed by an urgent commotion a few feet away. Alarmed, the kids swung round.

A fat man in a burgundy sports jacket was clawing at his chest! The man's face was nearly as dark as his coat, and the veins on his neck stood out like blue rivers on a road map. Even from a distance the children could hear the desperate wind-through-a-ripped-bellows wheeze as he tried to drag in fresh breath. The man lost consciousness and toppled from his chair like a felled oak, sending a landslide of cutlery and cups crashing to the floor. A woman behind him screamed.

The world seemed to drop into slow motion for Eleanor. A team of doctors armed with a portable defibrillator sprinted towards the victim. Bystanders reeled back in panic to let them through. In moments, the doctors had his shirt open and defib paddles pressed against his gray-skinned chest. Eleanor noticed with extraordinary clarity the texture of one doctor's frayed shirt collar and the way his muscles twisted like flexing knots beneath his skin.

She was astonished and appalled by the victim's aura. Its natural hue must have been a deep wine red, but that was almost entirely obscured by choking veins of whiteness. Energy radiating from his body was pulsing in and out like an electrocuted anemone as the man's life hung in the balance. Just from looking at his aura, Eleanor could tell that his heart was in spasm. He would be dead within minutes. As she watched, the writhing, white streaks gobbled up the remaining red patches with terrifying velocity. To Eleanor, the battle in the man's aura was just as real as the one on the floor as the doctors raced to save his life. The white veins seemed so vivid, popping out at her like white maggots. She felt like she could almost reach out and nip them away with her fingertips…

A high-pitched whine jerked Eleanor out of her trance. It was the charging of the defibrillator. There followed a meaty *thunk* as the emergency team delivered a jolt to the man's chest. He arched like a bow, then fell back to the floor, still slack.

"Again!" one doctor ordered, then, "CLEAR!"

The second shock produced the same flatline. Eleanor saw that the diner's body of light was ghostly now, little more than a watercolor tint beneath the throbbing white. The doctor with the frayed collar threw a grim glance at his colleagues, shook his head the tiniest of degrees.

Then Eleanor felt…a tug. A weird tingling in her fingertips, almost as if an unseen force were pulling them *towards* the white maggots. While everyone else's attention was on the doctors, Eleanor made a tiny gesture in the direction of the parasites…and the man's colors brightened like fanned embers!

Emboldened, Eleanor pinned her attention on the wormlike rays. Under the tabletop she twisted her fingers together as if she really were trying to tear away a nest of snakes. Incredibly, the pit of white vipers retreated like they were being driven back by a raging fire. Eleanor pressed her advantage. Behind the blankness she could make out burning colors and knew she needed to draw them out like bright handkerchiefs from a magician's sleeve. Out they came and within heartbeats—literally—the diner's halo had begun to stabilize.

On the floor the man coughed, then stirred with a moan. The crash team snapped instantly back into action, checking their patient's vitals, then rolling him over into the recovery position. Eleanor felt a wave of fatigue spill through her and slumped down into her chair like a broken doll. The man's aura still pulsed ominously around the edges, but there were healthier sparkles of cherry building up in its watery depths, growing stronger with every beat.

Across the table, Cody and Spencer were trading shaky smiles of relief while Lisa comforted the high-strung Tammy. Eleanor was trembling also, but for entirely different reasons. She didn't trust herself to meet anyone's gaze. *Somehow* she had just helped to save a man's life.

Ellie's previous fears clutched at her again. She felt like everyone else in the room knew, and if she looked up now she would find everyone else staring at her in open-mouthed disbelief. Would they think her a freak? Some kind of savior? It was all just so…frightening and…overwhelming. She had used auras to save someone. Maybe she was going to be able to help people after all—*and* do it in her own way.

Eleanor looked up, grinned. None of her friends had noticed anything after all. Eleanor would be able to come to terms with this incredible revelation at her own speed. She sighed.

That was when she looked back towards the stricken diner and saw the doctor with the frayed collar staring directly at her with an expression of fixed bewilderment etched onto his face.

CHAPTER 4

The Lost Mother

When Koemi arrived home, at first she didn't even realize anything was wrong.

There was nothing amiss in the little *genkan* vestibule where she removed her shoes, as tradition dictated, then drew back the *fusuma* door into the house itself. Everything was as it should be in the long, central passageway, and she paused for a moment to savor the fragrance drifting in from outside: cherry blossoms, *susuki* grass and ligustrum trees. Koemi and her mother, Tsukiko, lived on a quiet, detached plot on the edge of Narusawa Village, a tiny hamlet that bordered on Aokigahara Jukai. It was a peaceful, rustic place, though touched with a subtle taint of sadness. Everyone who lived there was aware of the grim notoriety the nearby forest had gathered in the past few decades.

Koemi laughed for just a second, splitting the silence down the middle. She couldn't keep in her delight as she recalled Moriko and Katsu's faces gleaming with joy. Koemi had run all the way back from the forest just to feel the wind on her face and the rush of blood through her body! Her heart still drummed happily in her chest.

Giggling, Koemi skipped along the corridor and slid back the translucent paper *shōji* door into the living room. There, for the first time, she frowned. Not in alarm—not yet. There was just a tiny dimpling of the brow as she saw the low table where she and Tsukiko perched on neat *zabuton* cushions to eat. It wasn't set for their meal, which was strange. Now that she came to consider her surroundings she couldn't detect any scents of cooking either. Hadn't her mother returned from the hotel yet?

Tsukiko's shifts as a maid often meant that she worked odd hours, especially when she was offered overtime during a busy tourist season. That said, she'd talked of a special meal to celebrate Koemi's birthday followed by an invigorating nature ramble around the foot of Mount Fuji. Tsukiko was no longer the light, airy soul she had once been, but she wouldn't simply forget her daughter's birthday. Hopefully her mother hadn't gone wandering aimlessly around shops to avoid coming back to face the house on her own. It was draining for Koemi to keep her mother's mood constantly buoyed up, though she didn't resent the labor for a moment.

The tatami mats that covered the floor in a complex, interlocking pattern crunched very softly as Koemi crept back into the hall. She tiptoed to the sliding door that screened in her mother's bedroom. Peeking through the doorway, she glimpsed Tsukiko's mantle of glossy, black hair fanned out across the pillow and knew that her mother had simply taken a nap upon returning. She must have been exhausted after the toil of cleaning lodges all day. Hoping she would awake refreshed and recharged, Koemi withdrew.

When she reached the kitchen, she became just that faintest bit unsettled—*something* was needling away at her just below the threshold of her attention, like the hum from a faulty lamp in an otherwise silent room. Then she saw a birthday card propped up on the work surface, her name scrawled out on the front in her mother's distinctive hand, and warm feelings filled her chest.

It stung a little that Tsukiko wasn't awake to make a fuss over Koemi and perhaps wouldn't be able to join in with the plans they'd made, but not to worry. Koemi understood that with only Tsukiko's wage to support them, her mother had to work all the extra hours she was offered and fretted terribly when she only reaped minimum pay. Koemi resolved to make Tsukiko a calming bowl of tea so that would be the first scent she woke to. In Koemi's mind, she'd already received the best birthday present she could have wished for—Moriko and Katsu's lives.

Koemi scampered back into the living room, planning to rummage around in the *chadansu* cabinet for tea-making paraphernalia, but instead, she abruptly halted. The photos on top of the cabinet had all been laid facedown.

There was nothing solemn about Koemi. She was a girl who laughed from the moment she opened her eyes in the morning until the time her head hit the pillow again in the evening. However, her expression was uncharacteristically sober as she picked up the fallen photos and peered into the smiling, frozen faces of her father and two sisters.

When her power to channel the healing laughter had first emerged, an almost indescribable sense of peace had settled around Koemi's heart. On the occasion when she'd met her first despairing businessman in the depths of Aokigahara Jukai and lifted his spirit back towards life, she *knew* that she would meet her lost family again: Kenji, Kamiko and Rika. Dead they might have been, but gone they were not. Their presence was like the breath in her lungs or the blood roaring through her heart. Intimate, eternal.

This was a tranquillity that Tsukiko struggled to find. Their loss loomed like a vast shadow across her life. Still, Koemi was always there to help her and would never give up. Recently, she was convinced they were making progress. With each passing day, she was sure that the ice in her mother's smiles thawed just a little bit more. However, she understood that the path to recovery was a winding trail, not a golden highway, and Tsukiko would sometimes have to go to bed early and turn family photos to the wall.

With a little sigh, Koemi tracked back to the bedroom to be with her mother.

■ ■ ■ ■ ■

Koemi stood over Tsukiko, fondly watching her sleep, then dipped in to place a tender kiss on her mother's cheek. As she stepped into the lean, her big toe nudged something lying on the mat. She heard it roll under the bed with a distinct whirring tick. Frowning, Koemi knelt down to peer under the *raku* platform after the offending object. She squinted. It was small and round and tubular and... Koemi gasped.

It was a plastic pill bottle. An *empty* plastic pill bottle.

All the skin down Koemi's neck ran with ice-cold stitches, like she'd been spiked by a hundred freezing acupuncture needles at once. She leapt to her feet and threw back the bedsheets in one jagged, desperate motion.

"Mother! Mother!" she cried, shaking Tsukiko by the shoulders.

But Tsukiko was totally unresponsive. Her head lolled on her shoulders like a balloon tied to a stick. Her flesh was clammy and her breathing...her *breathing...* Koemi couldn't *hear* her breathing even though she was mere inches away.

Koemi abandoned her post by the bed and sprinted for the phone on the hall table by the front door. Poorly adhered tatami mats skidded beneath her panicked feet and she almost fell twice before she snatched up the handset and stabbed wildly at its keys. Once the call was made there was nothing else to do except dash back to Tsukiko. On the way, Koemi noticed the envelope she'd brought with her from the kitchen sitting discarded on the bedside table. A horrible thought struck the girl like a blow to the solar plexus. Fingertips trembling, Koemi fumblingly tore open her birthday card.

Inside she found a one-page letter, which read in an unsteady scrawl, "Dearest Koemi, you are my most precious flower, but I cannot bear this pain any longer..."

■ ■ ■ ■ ■

In the ambulance, Koemi didn't dare hold her mother's hand too tightly.

Tsukiko's palm was limp as an autumn leaf, and she looked heartbreakingly frail. Her skin was so pale against the lurid orange pillow of the gurney that Koemi feared she might wring the life out of her just by squeezing. Panic fluttered like a bird trapped inside her chest. She tried to calm herself. Tsukiko's skin might have been ashen, but at least it remained warm.

As the wailing ambulance hurtled along the dark, country

roads, Koemi couldn't help but blame herself. If only she hadn't been dwelling on her successes with Moriko and Katsu, then perhaps she might have sensed something was wrong the instant she danced into the hallway. If only, if only…

The two uncommunicative paramedics sat up front, still wearing the white hardhats that they hadn't removed during the entire emergency. They'd even paused to laboriously remove their boots rather than leaping immediately into action to scoop up the stricken victim. Koemi had begged them to hurry, but they had ignored her strained pleas. There was protocol to observe. Koemi desperately wished she lived in a country where EMTs weren't bound by a thicket of regulations that rendered them little more than glorified drivers. In Japan, even if they were fully qualified, paramedics weren't allowed to as much as apply a Band-Aid.

Neither man said a word now. One drove while the other filled out paperwork on a clipboard across his lap, riding the jounce of the vehicle over potholes. The normally carefree Koemi found a strange anger rising up inside her at the paramedics' casual indifference. What had become of the world when ambulance men didn't care?

For a fleeting instant, Koemi thought she heard a malevolent chuckling. She whipped around, but of course there was nothing there. Just the white metal panels of the vehicle. Still Koemi's heart raced in fear. Suddenly, Tsukiko let vent a single weak moan.

Koemi yelped and dived across to the gurney. "Mother, it's Koemi! I'm here! Please stay with me, Mommy. Please don't go…"

■ ■ ■ ■ ■

Koemi sat in an anonymous hospital waiting room, reading and rereading Tsukiko's note. She obsessively analyzed the meager sentences to see if they contained any clues as to why she hadn't been able to help her mother like she could the lost souls in Aokigahara. Soon the words were swimming before her eyes as her tears splashed on the page, and it became impossible to read any more. The paper was quickly reduced to a soggy rag in her hands.

Suddenly the doctor was there, and he was telling her that they'd pumped Tsukiko's stomach, and she was going to be all right! On impulse, Koemi hugged the stern, grandfatherly physician, and he awkwardly patted her back while she sobbed with relief.

Tsukiko was actually sitting up in bed when they ushered Koemi into the tiny recovery area. A very young nurse in a knife-sharp uniform sat on a stool near the door and kept a watchful eye over proceedings.

Tsukiko's face was horribly puffy, with dark bags under her eyes, but despite the ravages of the stomach pump she'd regained a ruddy glow in stark contrast to the deathly pallor she'd possessed in the ambulance. Tears flowed freely. There was only one thing on Koemi's mind: she hadn't tried hard enough to stop her mother from falling into grief. She wouldn't make that mistake again.

"Mother, let's do some of our laughing," she urged in a voice that only Tsukiko could hear. "I know it's difficult, but if you just take my hand you'll be able to feel the joy flowing through you again, I promise. I'm getting so much better at this, every day in Aokigahara…"

Her mother's eyes were starry slits focused somewhere in the distance, but now her attention abruptly came back into the room. She brushed her daughter's lips with her paper-dry fingertips to halt the tumble of words.

"Aokigahara Forest?" she asked. Her voice was a husk of its former self. "I remember walking there when you were little...with you and your father and your sisters..."

Koemi could sense an approaching crack in her mother's voice as her reminiscences strayed towards dangerous territories. She quickly leapt in:

"We'll go back there soon. It will be so peaceful. But now let's think of a funny memory together!"

"Not now, my blossom," Tsukiko begged weakly, her eyelids flickering. "Later, perhaps... Let your mother rest..."

Tsukiko's neck relaxed and her head rocked back against the pillow. Within moments, the cadence of her breath had softened into slumber. Koemi sat cross-legged on the floor and watched her mother, her lips pressed together, trying by sheer force of will to calm the wings still beating within her chest.

■ ■ ■ ■ ■

The hospital kept her mother until the following morning; she was briskly discharged with little ceremony just before lunchtime. They hailed a taxi from the dreary reception concourse and took the slow ride home. Against all expectations, Tsukiko did seem oddly peaceful. She gazed out of the window at the blue shadow of Mount Fuji with clear eyes and an unfurrowed brow. In preceding months, even when things had been going well, there had been an anxious tension to Koemi's mother, a constant, barely detectable prickle of unease just below the surface. It kept Koemi from ever properly relaxing, but that edginess had completely evaporated. It was as if this close shave with death had given her mother a new appreciation of how precious her existence was.

Tsukiko's serenity persisted throughout the rest of the day. Little by little Koemi started to allow herself to hope that maybe—*just maybe*—they had put the worst of the darkness behind them. By the evening, Koemi had built up enough confidence to make fresh plans with her mother.

"Tomorrow morning I'll make you a traditional breakfast just as you like it," she began as casually as she could as they both sat on her mother's bed. Tsukiko was under the sheets, Koemi on the edge, and they were playing checkers on a little magnetic travel board. "Salted salmon fillet, sour plum and pickles with *natto* on the side," Koemi listed. "Afterwards we'll take the bus into town and go to the market—I've phoned the hotel and made an excuse, so they won't expect you in for a day or two. When we come back, we'll just go and sit in the garden and laugh and talk. Is…that okay?"

Koemi's voice was as bright as ever, yet she couldn't completely eliminate the note of pleading from her tone. "In a few days, we'll go walking in Aokigahara," she continued. "And we'll really talk about Father and Kamiko and Rika, and all the ways they made us happy…made us laugh…"

Koemi felt the whole world pull tight around her. This was a very risky strategy, actually to delve into the source of her mother's grief in order to heal her. Koemi held her breath, waiting agonizingly for her mother's reaction.

Tsukiko looked at her daughter and said very honestly, "I'd like that a lot." Then she smiled for the first time in months.

The bird trapped inside Koemi's chest finally flew free, and a joyful warmth instantly replaced its fluttering.

Koemi and her mother embraced, their laughter mingling.

It was half past two in the black depths of the morning when Koemi jerked awake. Her senses were instantly alive. The air seemed filled with a terrible electricity, and it took a long moment before she realized what had roused her: *the front door had just slammed.* She'd heard it in her dreams.

Koemi didn't bother to dress. She launched herself off her bed and down the hall like she was trying to take flight. One snatched sideways glance told her what she already knew—Tsukiko's room was deserted—as she plucked a coat off a peg in the vestibule and dove out into the vast, whispering night beyond.

The chill air sliced straight through the thin silk of Koemi's pajamas, but she paid it no heed. She sprinted as if the hordes of the demonic *oni* from folklore were at her back. She sprinted in the direction of Aokigahara Jukai.

When she had run back the previous day, Koemi's laughter had echoed, bell-like, all around the fields and trees. Now, she was cursing herself for her naiveté. She realized with a bitter jolt that her mother's recovery had been a sham. Tsukiko's serenity hadn't been born out of any renewed enthusiasm for life. It was the dreamlike acceptance of someone floating through the final hours until they could slip free of life's chains. Talking about Aokigahara had just given Tsukiko the perfect destination for her suicide.

Koemi's lungs burned and her legs screamed. She swiftly became lightheaded. This must have been why she imagined that a spectral presence was keeping pace with her, hissing its way over rocks and under bushes, mocking her with a low, gurgling snicker. The presence was like the personification of all her fears. If she didn't push her young body beyond its limits, then Tsukiko would be lost...

It was enough, but barely. She reached the black, looming tree line of Aokigahara weak, wobbling and close to collapse. She had managed to catch up to Tsukiko and saw her up ahead. However, even before she had a chance to call out, the ghostly white figure of her mother vanished into the jaws of the forest.

CHAPTER 5

Drawn to Kill

Harata liked being a cat best.

In the days that followed the revelation of her powers she tentatively tested out all her new abilities. Leaving her body for real was a truly terrifying experience because she knew that it really was her living, breathing self left down there on the bedroll. For that reason, she only dabbled in spirit-flying.

Slipping free of her flesh worked exactly as it had in the dreams, except now she could choose when it happened. There was a sort of state of mind that gave rise to the *tug*. She had to close her eyes and relax her whole body. That was where the tug lived, on the very edge between sleep and wakefulness.

Harata found that she could pluck at it like she was teasing out a thread from a blanket, then *whoosh*, away she would go, up, up and away! Doing this in real life rather than just in a dream, however, could feel very unnerving! So, for the time being she kept out of the skies.

What she did take to with relish was entering the minds of other creatures. She didn't dare consider invading a person's mind. Entering into someone's thoughts was an overwhelming prospect for an imaginative girl like Harata. What would she find? How would it feel? Would *they* be able to sense *her?* Would she be able to see images in their minds, enter their dreams? There was a dizzying array of questions she wasn't ready to address yet. Not yet, and maybe never.

Instead, she started small. There was a family of brown mice living in her bedroom wall. Her spirit body didn't have any mass, so she was able to worm her way effortlessly through a crack and into the dusty blackness beyond. She immediately rushed towards two tiny, bright eyes and—*zap!*—she was inside a mouse. Following that, she spent a highly disconcerting hour snuffling around in the cramped space behind her walls, sometimes scampering vertically, sometimes upside down, until she was thoroughly disoriented. This was only made worse by experiencing it all through mice senses: half blind, yet with ears sensitive enough to hear the slightest scratch of a beetle three walls away!

It was a fascinating lesson in how other creatures saw the world, but not one she cared to repeat. Next, she somewhat ambitiously entered the mind of a pigeon soaring high above Lahore, but the bird's spinning, wheeling, darting attention made her feel so nauseous that she quickly sprang back into her own body. Next she tried—very briefly—to squeeze into an ant walking in a troop along her balcony, but its tiny mind was locked on to that single activity and it felt like driving a car with a crowbar through the steering wheel. Also, peering out through its compound eyes was like looking through two jewels.

Finally, she scaled back up and dove into her pet cat, Spotty. This turned out to be the perfect balance of the familiar and the strange. Spotty moved so easily, so fluently, that it was as if she were wearing a magical, acrobatic fur suit. Nature experienced from within was an incredible feeling.

When Harata was inside these animals, she wasn't merely a passenger, nor did she control them exactly (and wouldn't have wanted to, as it was too close to exploitation for comfort). She did find that she could *suggest* things to them, gently nudging their little minds in this direction or that. She used this technique to tour the neighborhood at night while riding around inside Spotty.

It was exciting to see a version of the city she knew so well while slinking through marvellous dark nooks and crannies, under rotten cardboard boxes, up across gutters. She and Spotty scaled the levels of the Old City, bathing in the stew of scents, sounds and images that only a predator's heightened senses could pick up. For Harata, looking through Spotty's sharp eyes was like peering through a filthy window that had been cleaned for the very first time. To the cat, the whole world looked like a climbing frame, exciting tiers and ladders to race across in the pursuit of his tiny prey. Harata felt a pang of guilt for the cousins of the mouse who Spotty hunted, but this was just the cycle of life. It was how the natural world replenished and revitalized itself.

Being inside Spotty also brought home to Harata how predators could become prey in a flash. Once, as the cat padded across an open stretch of grass in a nearby park, he was suddenly confronted by a pack of huge, black dogs. Spotty instantly hissed, arching his back as his fur flared up in fear.

Even though she was safe back in her room at home, Harata felt Spotty's acute vulnerability as the five stinking, hellish-looking beasts loomed over him. The street dogs were mangy, horribly scarred and twisted by old injuries, quite possibly driven mad by some disease. That must have explained why their eyes appeared so red in the darkness, bloodshot and strangely staring. The leader, a bullmastiff, rumbled low in its throat, hot saliva falling in sheets around its bared fangs.

Even though she found the dogs disgusting, Harata told herself that they were only animals, and she needed to experience *all* sorts of minds in her journey of discovery. Also, she wanted to give Spotty a chance to escape. So, leaving the cat to scurry quickly to safety up a tree, Harata threw herself out of his mind and flew towards the bullmastiff. These beasts couldn't hurt her spirit form, so there was no reason to be worried...

Harata bounced back.

Some *barrier* prevented her from entering the bullmastiff. Left inexplicably dizzy by this collision, Harata caught her bearings. She made another run at the dog...only to be deflected again! Worried and confused, Harata attempted to enter a couple of the other hounds but was similarly defeated. Worse still, these jarring recoils left her spirit vision blurred and smoky. Soon she could no longer stand the disconnection from her body and instantly flashed back home.

She sat up in her bedroom and tried to shake the confusion from her senses. In that last moment before she'd left the park, she had noticed that the dogs weren't even chasing after Spotty. They simply remained waiting in the shadows, silently watching.

Not long after that, Spotty himself appeared on her balcony, mewing plaintively, seemingly none the worse for his ordeal. Harata let him in and rubbed the cat under the chin until he purred happily. It appeared that her spirit form wasn't able to enter creatures with diseased or damaged minds, though that didn't really explain why she had heard distant laughter echoing in *her* mind whenever she'd rebounded from the dogs.

■ ■ ■ ■ ■

Harata didn't breathe a word of her bizarre experiments to anyone else. Not to family, not to friends, not even to gentle Syed. It just wasn't safe until she knew exactly what she was dealing with. She had no idea what might happen if one of her brothers—or, merciful Allah, even Papa!—blundered in on her laid out on her bedroll, lolling like a rag doll. She might have woken up in a hospital bed—at best. Worst of all, she might have come to with a holy man looming over her, reciting verses from the Qur'an in an attempt to drive out evil spirits!

She bought a padlock from the market. It might have been difficult to explain to Kedar why she needed to lock herself away, but she felt she could probably convince everyone that she needed more privacy as she was now nearing womanhood.

The one flaw in this campaign of secrecy, however, was Tahir. Since the incident with his sunglasses he'd become a constant, bullying thorn in her side. More often than not, the moment she lay down and began to enter the spirit body mind state, he would come hammering on her bedroom door, demanding to know what she was doing.

Harata could get him to leave temporarily if she shouted back that she was performing optional prayers, but this only gained her a brief respite. Invariably Tahir would be back at mealtime, berating her for her interest in American films, or how she brazenly ran around in the streets, or any number of other alleged crimes against her country, purity or family.

In the past months, Tahir's behavior had become increasingly aggressive and secretive. He'd hang around the house at odd times during the day. He'd go out for hours and hours at night with new friends whom he never brought home. He claimed he was going out to work, but Harata knew for a fact that he'd been fired from his job at the building site due to laziness. Sometimes he didn't come back for days and then would pick fights with everyone except Kedar upon his return.

A more observant father might have commented upon these dark notes creeping into his son's life, but as long as it didn't intrude upon his own contentment, Kedar just dismissed Tahir's surly machismo as "growing pains." Harata quickly learned to spot the restlessness that foreshadowed Tahir's storming out of the house, and she rescheduled her spirit experiments accordingly. Still, it was disturbing to see how Tahir had transformed from the comical, carefree boy she had once known into this unpredictable, rage-filled stranger.

■ ■ ■ ■ ■

After the worrying interlude with Spotty and the dogs, Harata decided she needed a new perspective on her growing abilities and their limitations. The time had come. She had just been putting off the inevitable anyway... She had to fly.

In the end, this turned out to be a bit of an anticlimax (if flying free of your body out across one of the most vibrant cities on Earth could ever be dismissed that way!). The techniques she had so painstakingly developed in her dreams finally clicked, and when she shook free of her physical body, she was immediately able to shoot off through the walls of her cramped life and out into the infinite blue spaces beyond.

It was a warm, clear, spring day as Harata soared over the carpet of streets and sparkling domes. Wonder thrilled through every fiber of her being. If everybody could experience like this the place where they lived, then surely much of the hate, anger and injustice in the world would simply melt away.

Flying up so high over everyone she knew, Harata began to wonder what she should do with these powers. She was not a hero in a movie, but like them she now had an opportunity to use extraordinary abilities for the good of all. There must have been some way she could help others…but how?

She spent the next hour crisscrossing the city as she mulled over this conundrum. However, feeling the air flowing through her spirit form was like gulping down a drink of ice water with her entire body, and soon she found her mind drifting. It was just too big a problem for her to solve on her own. Should she look for missing persons? Spend her time searching for crimes, then run and tell the police what she'd seen? No one would believe her. She could save cats trapped up trees and locate lost sunglasses, but that was all she could say with any certainty right now. Perhaps inspiration would come later. After all, there was no rush. She had all the time in the world.

■ ■ ■ ■ ■

Harata heard the first cracks as she was completing the long, shallow arc that would take her back towards Mall Road. A burst of sharp pops rising up from the compound of the Lahore High Court. It sounded a bit like bubble wrap being squeezed, though Harata assumed it was just an exhaust back-firing, which was so common in this city of aged cars. That was when she heard the screams.

Harata didn't have skin to go cold or flesh to crawl, but as she angled herself towards the High Court, some part of her certainly cringed with dread. Even peering directly down into the compound, it was difficult to work out exactly what was going on. Ragged shouts continued as panic-stricken men and women dashed back and forth, desperately trying to find cover as a group of figures in black strode unhurriedly amongst them, calmly lining up shrieking targets...then mercilessly gunning them down. Already many bodies lay twisted on the paving stones.

Appalled, Harata could only stare at the unfolding terror, her horror intensified by her feelings of utter impotence. She could no more flash down and save those people than a ghost could. It made a mockery of her aspirations to help the world. She was bodiless, powerless, and damned merely to watch the horror.

Although sirens were beginning to wail out across the city, it was clear they would arrive far too late. Already the gunmen were disappearing into the crowds, throwing off their black garb and running down alleyways or under bridges. Harata's powers became an unexpected curse as her keen spirit sight picked out red pools trickling away into cracks in the pavement.

In horror and shame, she vanished back home.

■ ■ ■ ■ ■

The attack dominated news bulletins for the rest of the week. The story was simple, but the ramifications were seismic. The gunmen belonged to an extremist Wahabbist terror group whose targets were all lawyers from Pakistan's Shia Muslim minority.

After that fateful day when the Twin Towers had fallen in New York City, the Americans and their allies had come and laid fiery waste to their enemies in Afghanistan. However, when the Taliban were expelled from their strongholds, they spilled over the border into neighboring Pakistan. Political and religious violence in Harata's country had been growing ever since.

The victims of this latest attack had been chosen individually; this was revealed by the lone gunman whom the authorities managed to arrest, though that was the extent of the intelligence they managed to get from him. He was little more than a kid from a tiny village in Waziristan, the mountainous northwest region bordering Afghanistan, and he'd had no direct contact with the men who had masterminded the attacks. All his instructions had been delivered in a code he wouldn't reveal. The next day he was found hanging, dead, in his cell. Foul play was suspected.

The atrocity affected every member of Harata's family differently. Kedar sternly blamed the ISI, their government's secret service, then retreated to his study, refusing to look at any news that wasn't sports-related. Gentle Syed wept in hiding places that only Harata knew about, while her other brothers, Hamid, Jakeem and Rafiq, became furious, disbelieving and jaded, respectively. Harata herself, after having been so intimately involved in the horror, just felt numb. She couldn't get the images of the blood dripping from the paving stones out of her mind.

Strangely, Tahir, who would normally shout his blood-thirsty political views from the rooftops, became very withdrawn. In the days after the atrocities, he took to sitting cross-legged on the balcony, poring over any newspaper he could get his hands on. What was most puzzling, however, was that whenever Harata peered over his shoulder, he always seemed to be looking at the personal-ads page.

Tahir started going out with even more frequency after that and often came home with strange bags or unusual packages. He tried to keep them hidden from any prying eyes, and the packages always vanished from the house by the very next day, but Harata saw.

Harata chose the next time Tahir returned home late at night to ambush her brother in the hallway.

"Where have you been?" Harata hissed.

"Working," Tahir spat back, his expression instantly slamming closed.

"At this hour? Where?"

"I don't have to tell you anything…but I will just to shut you up. I'm serving at the McDonald's in Liberty Market—"

Harata cut him off. "McDonald's? *You?* I don't believe it!"

"You know nothing, filthy little rat. You'll all see how special I am soon enough!"

"What does that mean?" Harata pressed him. "Tahir, what are you talking about?"

But Tahir retreated towards the boys' bedroom, refusing to look her in the eye. Harata gnawed her lip. There was no other option. She had to alert Kedar.

■ ■ ■ ■ ■

"Papa, I need to talk," she told Kedar as he was arranging himself eagerly in his favorite chair before their aging, blurry television.

"Be quick, daughter, can't you see the Test Match is about to start?"

Harata took a moment to collect her thoughts, then plunged in.

"Papa, it is Tahir. I'm worried he's fallen in with bad company! All of us have noticed the change in him. Syed agrees, and Hamid and Jakeem, even Rafiq. Tahir is not the boy he once was!"

Kedar didn't react, his gaze fixed on the fuzzy images of cricket players dashing across the screen. Exasperated by his apathy, Harata pressed her case.

"Papa, PLEASE! It's important! You saw what happened at the High Court when young men turn to darkness! The horror of—"

"No!" Kedar bellowed, startling Harata. "No son of mine would entertain such thoughts, and that is the end of it. Don't stick your nose in men's business. It's unseemly and disrespectful. Go now and never pester me with this women's gossip again!"

Harata set her jaw in mute, grinding frustration, but she knew there was nothing left to say. Kedar was as stubborn as he was pious. She would have to bring him incontrovertible proof of Tahir's misdeeds before he would deign to intervene.

She stalked off to do her own detective work.

■ ■ ■ ■ ■

The next day, when Tahir skulked off to his latest mysterious rendezvous, Harata was close behind. On the street it wasn't so hard for Harata to remain hidden. The crowds milling along the narrow throughways of Andheron Shehr were exceedingly dense, and after years as a tomboy rioting through the markets with her friends, Harata was far more used to surfing the waves of bodies than her brother. True, occasionally she was forced to sacrifice stealth for speed and lost sight of Tahir, but that was when her special advantages came into play. She simply stepped out of the flow for a moment, into a doorway, and projected her mind to locate her target again.

In this manner, she deftly trailed Tahir all the way to the boisterous environs of the Liberty Market. He didn't head for any MacDonald's but scurried furtively through the throng to a traditional Lahori cafe. Inside, he swiftly took the spare seat at a table occupied by half a dozen watchful old men, in dark clothes and black skullcaps, who greeted him in a formal fashion. Terse words were exchanged while the old men kept their eyes on the bustling street outside.

There was simply no way Harata could get closer without being spotted, unfortunately. She was keen to eavesdrop, but the old men were crafty and had clearly chosen a table that afforded them sight lines in every direction. There wasn't even a secluded spot she could duck behind to "spirit walk." Harata resigned herself to the role of a spectator squinting from the cheap seats. Luckily, she had prepared for such an eventuality and fished out the battered camera she had borrowed from Syed. She quickly made like a tourist, happily clicking away while making sure that she snapped as many shots of the café as possible.

Even this was short-lived, though, as Tahir was soon pushing his chair away from the table and striding stiffly back out onto the street. Harata blinked. Her brother was now in possession of a canvas bag that he carried with visible caution.

■ ■ ■ ■ ■

Harata visited a one-hour photo store to develop her snaphots, then, on the way back home, mulled over the implications of what she had seen. She was lost deep in thought as she drifted into their yard, which was why she didn't see the danger until it was far too late.

"How DARE you disobey me!" Kedar roared, causing Harata to almost leap out of her skin. He stood on the concrete step, hands on his hips.

"Your father has heard what they say in those American films you like so much," he told her. "So hear me now—you are GROUNDED!"

"Papa, NO! I have to tell you about Tahir's bag—"

"BE QUIET! You will stay in our home until you have proven you can be a respectable, obedient daughter!"

He rudely snatched the photos out of her hand and threw them over the fence, where they dropped into the gutter and slipped down the gaping drain.

■ ■ ■ ■ ■

Tahir didn't talk to anyone that night, nor during the following morning. While Kedar and Harata's other brothers bumbled around over breakfast rituals, Harata watched Tahir like a hawk. He was far too preoccupied to register her attention and just sat staring into his bowl, chewing mechanically. After about ten minutes of this, he abandoned his plate with a grimace and abruptly quit the table. He rooted about on the floor by Kedar's chair to locate the day's paper, then scurried out onto the balcony to scan it in the sun. Everything about his behavior had become suspicious.

Harata waited until she was certain that Tahir was engrossed by the paper, then tiptoed swiftly out towards the boys' room. The canvas bag was tucked under a blanket beside Tahir's bedroll. Harata hissed with frustration. Tahir had lashed twine around the handles so that the only way to peek inside would be to sever it completely and betray her tampering. Harata sat back on her haunches, mind racing. Why was Tahir so agitated? He'd brought home similar ominous packages before, and they'd never affected him quite like this.

Options exhausted, Harata skipped back to the kitchen— just in time to notice Tahir go stiff. His whole body trembled on the balcony and he glanced up, his eyes meeting hers with a haunted look. The paper tumbled off his knees, and he fled. Alarm growing, Harata darted after her sibling. She heard the front door rattle, then slam.

"Tahir! Tahir! Wait. I have to go to the market, I'll walk with you—" she called out.

But it was already too late. "Where are you going, you miscreant?" Kedar barked. "Go to your room NOW!"

Full of hectic energy, Harata desperately tried to work out how to intercept Tahir. She ran her hands up and down her sides with nervous tension, only for her fingernails to catch on something hidden in her quilted jacket. One of the photos must have slipped out of the developer's envelope! Hope flared in her heart, then wavered just as swiftly. The picture she'd been left with was out of focus and utterly humdrum. She couldn't even see Tahir properly. There was no way this would ever convince Kedar.

In anguish, Harata stared so hard at the photograph that her eyes began to water. The image of the café swam and sparkled...which was when the new thing happened. She felt the telltale *tug*. Only this time it didn't slide her spirit out of her body. It drew her *inside* the photograph!

Harata suffered a moment of vertigo, as if she were falling through an open window in the floor, then she was there, back in the scene on the bustling sidewalk. Instinctively she knew she hadn't travelled in time or space. She was still in her bedroom, but the photograph was acting as some kind of total-recall device. Inside the picture her vision had a crystalline clarity, though there was a strange shimmer to the light, a bronzing around the edges of objects and people when she turned her head too fast, as if her memories were struggling to keep up.

She swept like a specter into the café and stood at the shoulder of the old men's leader as he casually pushed the canvas bag towards Tahir under the table. Though the wrinkles on his face proved that he must have been very elderly, this man still retained an inky black beard. Tahir accepted the bag with a stunned look, like he didn't quite believe what his hands were doing.

"I wish to serve the cause and make Allah proud," he stammered.

"That does you well, young friend," the man with the dark beard replied.

Tahir's face crumpled in doubt. "But how will I know what to do, when..." He trailed off weakly. "How will I know the names of—"

"The chosen," said the dark-bearded man quickly, firmly cutting him off, "will be supplied to you through the same code the soldiers of God have used in the past. We must be wary of our words here, Tahir, where anyone might overhear."

Tahir went pale, ashamed by his naiveté. He bent to secure the throat of the canvas bag and as he did so, for the sliver of a second, Harata caught her first glimpse inside. She saw the dull, gleaming butt of a revolver!

The horror of this revelation threw Harata out of the photo and her memory in a sick rush. It left her shaking back in her bedroom. She wanted to throw up, but she knew she had to remain in control—for her family, for the innocent potential victims, and for Tahir himself. But was she already too late?

She sprinted out into their living area. Kedar, Hamid, Jakeem and Rafiq were having a heated debate about cricket and barely noticed her entrance. The first thing she saw when she turned towards the balcony was the paper Tahir had been reading, discarded on the slatted floor. Her eyes snagged on the personal ads and the mark Tahir had ringed around one single name. It was circled with such force that his pen had actually torn through the page.

Harata ran into the boys' bedroom, her breath coming in painful, abbreviated stabs. The canvas bag with the gun was no longer under the blanket. She threw open all the cupboards and drawers in rapid succession. Nothing. It was now clear how elegantly simple yet horrible the terrorists' code really was. They just printed the names on their assassination list in the personal ads!

Harata was forbidden to leave the house, Tahir was on his way to commit murder, and the only proof she had to convince anyone were memories gleaned from magically travelling inside a photograph!

CHAPTER 6

Doctor Vance

"**Y**ou can see auras, can't you?" said the doctor with the frayed collar, blocking Eleanor's exit.

The girl froze, her expression congealing into a mask of distress. He'd found her. What was even more galling was that she wouldn't normally be allowed in the pediatrics supply closet. It was only because they were in the middle of Cody's surprise party that Nurse Ina had asked her to rustle up some up some fresh linen for tablecloths, because the staff were so rushed off their feet. It wasn't Cody's birthday, but after all the punishing medical procedures he'd had to put up with recently, Ellie and the other kids had got together and decided he deserved a pick-me-up. When they proposed their idea to the adults, everyone heartily agreed. Unfortunately, in the excitement of the party itself, Ellie had momentarily forgotten about her new nemesis...

She'd been successfully avoiding "Frayed Collar" for days now. In a hospital of this size it wasn't so hard if you kept your wits about you. More than once she'd spied him at the far end of a corridor but easily managed to slip behind some plants or escape through a conveniently placed stairwell. Now she was cornered in the most cramped space in the building with no method of escape.

"I… I don't know what you're talking about," Ellie stammered, trying to dodge past him. His hair was curly, brown and mushroomed in all sorts of unlikely directions, while the eyes peering from behind his wire-rimmed spectacles were very direct and bright green. He seemed full of an intense, fizzy, childlike energy.

Eleanor didn't know how he knew she was responsible for helping the heart-attack man, but she wasn't about to hang around and find out. Like most painfully shy people, Eleanor's immediate response to confrontation was to flee as fast as she could. But Frayed Collar was too quick on his feet and blocked her exit.

"You know exactly what I mean. I was with the crash team in the cafeteria, trying to resuscitate that heart-attack victim… You did something to help him."

"Please, I— I don't know who you are or what you're talking about. I'm—I'm only nine, my mom works in the hospital and it's school vacation, that's why I'm here," Eleanor babbled.

"Not before you tell me what you did. It's *really* important. You have to tell me."

"You're the ones who saved him, you said. You were on the crash team."

This was what Eleanor feared most: people crowding in around her, poking her with questions she didn't dare answer.

"If I was halfway across the room, then how do you know I helped him?" she blurted.

For some reason, Frayed Collar suddenly become extremely nervous.

"Because I've been secretly researching auric healing for the last ten years," he shyly confessed.

▨ ▩ ▪ ▩ ▨

In the immediate aftermath of the cafeteria episode, Eleanor had been swamped by a torrent of conflicting emotions: rushes of excitement and jabs of fear, hope, joy and doubt, sometimes all at once.

Eventually her mood slowly crystallized into cautious optimism. At least trips to Saint Rafael's could never be considered boring again. She now had a bunch of awesome new friends and a place to do her art without being disturbed. Most of all, there was this amazing new power to explore. Now she could do more than just look. She wasn't merely a bystander anymore. Every day she would find a corner in reception, the cafeteria or one of the other corridors to draw and investigate this extraordinary ability.

As before, she included her subjects' light bodies, but now she went a step further and tweaked those auras in the same way she had with the heart-attack man, gingerly exploring her ability. It was almost like an extension of drawing. She would be dabbing a swirl of turquoise on the page, then suddenly, instinctively know that the picture needed a splash of indigo to complete it. She lifted her hand off the pad towards the young woman who was her subject and gently, hesitantly caressed her colors. This caused a whole new shade of purple to bloom in her aura, almost as if Eleanor were using her pastel in the air!

It needed a patient eye and a lot of practice, but invariably Eleanor was told by her subjects how happy and calm they felt afterwards. Eleanor soon discovered that staff and patients alike would beckon her over and ask her to draw them. She became known to everyone around the hospital and welcomed wherever she wanted to camp out.

Rachel was amazed by these new pictures Eleanor produced during this period, and much later Eleanor discovered that her mother had secretly entered them into a prestigious young-person's art competition called the Golden Wings Scholarship.

Subtly, gradually, the atmosphere in the whole hospital started to improve. People smiled more, became less apt to snap or brood. Emboldened by her successes, Eleanor gradually began to heal patients in small, cautious ways—easing back pain for half an hour or dissolving a migraine.

To her immense sadness, however, the one person her interventions didn't seem to help was Cody. His cancer had proven resistant to conventional therapies, and Eleanor's visits to Saint Rafael's had coincided with a sharp downturn in his condition. He still had his good days, and all the kids took rambunctious advantage of those, but more and more Ellie would come into the ward to find him propped up in bed with barely enough energy to wave. Cody was relentlessly upbeat, but it was clear to everyone that he was getting weaker by the day.

No one would admit it, but that was surely why staff, patients and his family put so much effort into planning his party.

■ ■ ■ ■ ■

Eleanor stood with Dr. Frayed Collar and watched a clown juggle rubber chickens for an audience of kids, staff and visiting relatives. They both sipped orange juice from plastic cups while wearing crepe-paper party hats.

Everybody else in the ward was totally focused on the entertainment, so this was actually a very safe place to talk. Cody was howling with laughter. His face glowed with enjoyment. It was a warmth that radiated off of him until it seemed to suffuse the whole room. Eleanor felt like she was the only tense one there.

"It started when I was a teenager, a little older than you are now," said Frayed Collar. His real name was Logan Vance. He'd already explained how he'd been assembling a body of research on the healing potential of auras since medical school. Whenever he'd opened up to colleagues, he'd been ridiculed. He knew that if he published anything without irrefutable proof he'd be ostracized by the entire medical community. This was why he was still laboring away in obscurity at Saint Rafael's. He was brilliant enough to get a job anywhere he chose, but this position enabled him to investigate energy medicine in a dynamic clinical environment. He'd been waiting his whole career for someone like Eleanor to come along.

"My dad was ill a lot," Logan continued. "He had chronic kidney disease and was in and out of the hospital. But occasionally, I started to see…these shimmering colors around him. I was a very logical, fussy kid, so I just dismissed them at first. Then I began to see how the hues would change as his condition improved or declined. So, being that same logical, fussy guy, I started to plot them on a chart. When he died, I saw his colors eaten up by a white void…"

Logan paused, consumed by memories of that tragic event,

which had set the path for the rest of his life. In an effort to distract him, Eleanor gently touched his shoulder.

"Is...is that how you knew what was happening with the man in the cafeteria? Did you see his colors?"

Logan nodded, sipping his juice thoughtfully. "Do you know how you do it... the healing?" he asked. "It's incredibly rare, in my experience."

Eleanor lowered her gaze with embarrassment at how little she really understood. "That was the first time I'd ever done anything like that. I didn't even know you could..." She trailed off uncertainly.

"Influence human energy fields? Yes, I've studied a number of people who seemed to have that ability to actively use auras... I've never encountered someone able to do it as powerfully as you, Ellie. But..." Logan frowned as he clearly thought better of what he'd been about to say.

"What? Please tell me! I've never met anyone else who even saw the colors, let alone has been researching them! I...I want to know everything!"

"Well, I don't want to scare you...but I have another theory about the auras. I think it's one that could change the world..."

■ ■ ■ ■ ■

The moment Logan opened the door, the wind tore at Eleanor's clothes, whipping her hair across her face like a blinding hood as they stepped out onto the gray, flat space of the hospital roof. Logan grinned like a friendly mad professor and beckoned. He motioned for Eleanor to be quiet and to move as stealthily as possible. In puzzlement, she followed Logan as they tiptoed around the back of an AC vent unit, where they found a group of pigeons huddled inside its hollow casing. The birds cooed sleepily and shuffled on their impromptu perch but didn't take flight.

"I think wherever they used to roost must have had been lousy with industrial contaminants," Logan whispered to Ellie. "They all have environmentally induced tumors," he said sadly. "Look at their wings."

Eleanor saw that indeed the pigeons' feathers were distorted by ugly, asymmetrical outgrowths. What she had first taken to be healthy drowsiness in the birds was, in fact, the lethargy of disease.

"I want you to heal them," Logan continued in a totally matter-of-fact tone.

Immediately Eleanor started backing away in panic.

"I… I can't even stop someone's back pain for more than an hour! I'll hurt them…or worse. I don't want to be responsible for causing any creature pain. I can't, I'm sorry!" Before she could escape Logan grasped her firmly by the shoulders. He looked deep into her eyes. Logan's aura was deepest violet—the color she had come to associate with wisdom—and so intense it was almost black. Logan's aura was so strong it almost looked painted onto the air around him. It instantly inspired trust in Ellie.

"I've been waiting for this moment for years, researching, planning… You should see the office I've got crammed with files! I know you can do this, Ellie, with my help." His face dipped closer. "Can I tell you my secret? The idea that could change the world?" Eleanor nodded. "I think that aura manipulation is an innate human ability. All life is a system of interconnected electromagnetic fields, and since the body is an organized field of energy, it can transmit information from one body to another. If we just knew how, then anybody on earth could do it...Anybody!" Hope flared within Eleanor's chest. It was as if Logan could read her thoughts.

"Oh, yes! Yes! That's what I think too! How wonderful that would be... If *everyone* could see auras then we could heal the world, we could cure depression, we could—"

"But not until we understand fully how *you* do it, Eleanor," Logan interrupted her. "I know it's an awful burden to put on the shoulders of someone so young, but please, Eleanor—I have faith in you."

Eleanor turned very slowly, so as not to startle the birds, and focused her auric sight. The pigeons' halos were smaller, fuzzier and far less complex than people's, but the principles were the same. It was more difficult to manipulate their auras without her pad and pastels, but Logan was there to advise, constantly offering a commentary of crucial suggestions as Ellie's fingertips danced nervously in the air.

"Use the green, Ellie, bring that up! Green is the color of health, of life, of natural growth... Yes, yes! It's working!"

Eleanor did what she was told, and within moments she was rewarded with a verdant grass-colored light shining around the pigeons. It was exhilarating, so perfect. Logan grinned at her. Relief flooded through Ellie's body and she sagged down onto the sill of a boarded-up window.

"Will you teach me, Logan? Please? I've wanted so badly to help people, and now I finally might be able to!"

Logan's face became thoughtful, and he sat next to her.

"I will, but I have one condition before I agree...and it's a biggie. I've been laboring over this for most of my life, Ellie, in secret and silence...for fear that I'd never be able to work again if I talked about my ideas. *You* are the proof I need to convince everyone. Together, Eleanor, we can change the world… I can teach you all I know but, in exchange, I want us to go public about your ability." He paused. "At the end of the month."

This was a truly horrifying prospect. To be exposed not just in front of other kids but, ultimately, the entire world's media! However, if Logan could truly teach Ellie to heal people properly, well, wouldn't that be worth a little bit of anxiety on her part?

"Okay, let's do it," she agreed. "But we start with Cody first."

■ ■ ■ ■ ■

To Eleanor's delight, the first healing session with Cody went better than she ever could have imagined.

Cody greeted her sleepily as she crept into the private room where he'd been transferred when his condition worsened. Logan hovered in the doorway like a watchful angel.

"I can barely keep my eyes open. That's the chemo," Cody slurred.

His hair had fallen out about a week earlier, and he spent more of his time drowsing than awake. "Why don't you hang around 'til after I've had my nap? We can play on my Game Boy. You could draw me while I sleep, I don't mind."

Ellie opened her mouth to reply, but Cody had already started to snore softly through his nose. Logan flashed Ellie an encouraging smile and mouthed, "*Green aura.*"

Even though her stomach was churning Eleanor broke out her pad and set to work on her friend's ravaged colors. When Cody woke a short time later, he was ravenously hungry and full of irrepressible, vigorous energy like he hadn't felt for months. Walking alongside him, Ellie grinned all the way to the cafeteria.

■ ■ ■ ■ ■

After that, Eleanor and Logan's work accelerated exponentially as they raced towards the fateful day of the big reveal. (Logan had some friends in the media he could call on, though, naturally, he hadn't mentioned what it was all about!)

Logan presented Eleanor with a carefully chosen list of patients, along with notes on their ailments and the color therapies to try. Like a doctor, Eleanor made her rounds every morning, dropping in on her patients to continue her auric remedies under the guise of elaborate portraits in a totally new style. There was jolly Mr. Craven with liver failure, and Janice Peterson, who suffered from crippling arthritis and loved game shows. Tim Keel had been cut down by advanced stages of diabetes and had a twin sister who came to visit him every day at seven fifteen on the dot.

The list went on and on. Sometimes it was a daunting roll call, but Logan accompanied Ellie when he could, and it felt great to have someone there to rely on, someone to talk to and give her guidance. It was great not to feel alone anymore. Also, the results were nothing short of jaw-dropping. Every one of her charges responded with shining displays of health and renewed energy.

In her spare time Eleanor did her own research into auras online and at the local library. She was appalled by how much disinformation there was out there. It was all airy-fairy speculation and confusion. She did find one good book—a single battered copy that had fallen down a dusty gap between two shelves. It was written by an Italian man named Agostino, who explained how auras were fields of electromagnetic energy that surrounded the body of all living beings, and that, all the systems of the body- from the cardiovascular to the endocrine- possess their own unique vibrations. Different ailments could be healed by applying specific colors of corresponding vibrational energy. Although this book helped her, most of Agostino's advice was outdated, made obsolete by Logan's fresh research. Logan taught her never to be tentative but to tear boldly through sickly colors. It sometimes felt so close to vandalism that it was a thrill, like ripping off old wallpaper before you redecorate!

By infinitesimal degrees, Ellie started to look forward to their big announcement. Sure, it was terrifying, but she had finally realized the way in which she really wanted to help people: by being a teacher. If she could get through this, then she'd easily be able to stand in front of a class and teach in the future.

They continued to go out onto the roof. It was their special place where they could escape the sluggish, recycled air of the hospital corridors. Ellie continued to hone her skills on the pigeons, which flitted joyously about, scattering up higher and higher into the warm blue sky. They swooped and soared like Ellie's hopes and dreams. She couldn't recall a time in her life when she'd been happier.

■ ■ ■ ■ ■

Three days before they were due to reveal Eleanor's secret to the world, Cody collapsed.

When Eleanor arrived a few hours later, she discovered that he had been rushed into emergency surgery and was now in the recovery area, still extremely ill. She held a crisis meeting with Logan on their secret rooftop spot. The clouds above looked like a jumble of broken, gray slates.

"We have to go ahead, Ellie," Logan insisted. "Your powers are real, and we can't lose faith. This is too important to falter now, even with a terrible setback like this. We have to stay strong and keep the course..."

Eleanor paced back and forth, wringing her hands in anxiety.

"But it's not just Cody. Some of the other patients don't seem well either. I'm...just really frightened that this will undermine everything I want to teach people, and no one will listen!"

"Nonsense, Ellie—these things take time to perfect, like any new skill. The world will understand that. Plus, I've seen this time and again in my research. These peaks and troughs are typical of energy healing. At first you see great improvements, then a sudden crash, but it slowly builds back up into a full cure. It's part of the natural cycle, believe me. Cody will be fine, I promise. Just you wait and see."

Logan had a naturally soothing presence. It was what gave him such an effective bedside manner. She smiled shakily back at him, but she was masking how she really felt.

It was clear that Logan was protecting her by not revealing how badly she had failed. The one thing her friends on the kids' ward had taught her was that you had to be brave and face your fears. She needed to see the truth about Cody's condition, even if that meant going behind Logan's back.

■ ■ ■ ■ ■

"I need your help," Ellie whispered to Lisa and Tammy later that day.

Everybody on the ward was rattled after Cody's lapse, and tensions were running high. Haltingly, while skirting round some of the more incredible details, Ellie explained how she had been working with Logan to help Cody with her aura viewing. Lisa and Tammy knew Ellie now and knew that she would never lie about something as important as this. So both girls vigorously nodded in support, urging Ellie to continue.

"I...feel so responsible," Ellie muttered. "I have to find out what's really going on and if—*if* I've made Cody worse. I'm pretty sure that if I can get access to the computer at the nurses' station for a minute, I can look in Logan's notes and see if he's been hiding things about Cody's progress. I know his password. Somebody needs to draw the nurses away, though, and keep a lookout while I'm at the keyboard."

One glance at Lisa and Tammy showed what firm friends they really were.

■ ■ ■ ■ ■

They put their plan into action over lunch, when staff coverage on the ward was at its most diluted. It had been decided that because of her eyesight and the fact that she knew more about computers, Lisa would accompany Eleanor, who would actually work the screen. Tammy would act as their decoy. At twelve thirty on the dot, Tammy exploded out of the stairwell door in a storm of tears, panic and flying pigtails.

"Help! Help! There's a man in a wheelchair who's fallen on the lower landing! I'm not strong enough to help him up, and I think he may be really hurt! I'll need both of you—PLEASE! *Quickly.*"

It turned out—not to anyone's surprise—that Tammy was extremely good at pretending to be hysterical!

The moment the door clashed behind Billy, Ina and Tammy, Ellie and Lisa darted for the nurses' station. Ellie threw herself at the seat. Her fingers rattled over the computer's keyboard as she feverishly worked. The computer, however, proved maddeningly uncooperative, chugging, freezing unexpectedly and throwing out a blizzard of unfamiliar menus at every keystroke.

"Come on, come on," Ellie muttered. "Damn, where is it? Where do they keep doctors' notes?"

At her shoulder, Lisa babbled nervously.

"Your new friend, the doctor guy. I like him, but he has just the weirdest aura, doesn't he? It just doesn't look right, like it's fake almost, or painted on."

Agostino's book had explained how blind or partially sighted people were able to sense color as a result of energy vibrations transmitted within the body. It meant that their perception of colors was often better than their sighted companions.

"Yeah, a bit," murmured Ellie, preoccupied with the screen. "But that's only because he has such a potent life force, I think."

"Oh. Okay… There's this other thing, though—really odd. Maybe it's just because I don't see so well, and my ears are more highly attuned, but—promise you won't make fun—sometimes when I look at Logan's aura, I hear this faraway…laughter…"

But Ellie had stopped listening. She was just staring at the screen. There was no trace of Logan anywhere in the database.

No listing of him. Not as a doctor, not as anything. He simply wasn't there—*at all.* Eleanor jerked her fingers off the keyboard as if she'd received an electric shock. It felt like the walls were closing in on her like a trash compactor. Logan wasn't in the database. Her chest was tightening. She had to get out! Had to breathe!

Without another word to the baffled Lisa, Eleanor lurched out of the ward.

■ ■ ■ ■ ■

Eleanor fell through the battered steel door and out onto the roof. Blindly, she stumbled to the spot where the pigeons roosted, but when she rounded the corner she had to suppress a gasp. Their bodies littered the gritty asphalt surface in a trail of ragged, dark humps, beaks open, legs frozen, all dead...because of her...*because of Logan.*

Eleanor was worried that she might pass out. With an enormous effort she calmed herself. Logan was an imposter. He wasn't a doctor, wasn't even a friend.

Everything he had told her, all his advice, his research, his encouragement... Lies!

The truth came crashing down upon Ellie like a mountain falling. Every time she'd ripped through sickly auras and felt like she was doing damage, *she had been!* He'd *wanted* her to fail, to harm people with her powers, to expose her to the world's media as a lethal freak of nature. Had he done it *all* just to discredit her? Why? She was only a child—a shy, thin girl in an undistinguished New York hospital. It made no sense. What could he possibly have hoped to gain from deceiving her in such an elaborate way?

A shiver ran through Eleanor. Her spine snapped straight. None of that mattered. She stared at the sad, lonely tufts of feathers stirred by the breeze. Those tufts had once been living, breathing creatures. She knew what she had to do.

■ ■ ■ ■ ■

Eleanor's sneakers screamed on the shining floor as she dashed back onto the ward. She realized something was horribly amiss when Nurse Ina didn't immediately ask what was wrong. The big woman's eyes were brimming wet, and she dabbed at them with a pink Kleenex from her sleeve. Ellie went cold.

"You'd better go in and see your friend, baby. I'm so sorry but his consultant thinks…well, Cody might not be…with us in the morning."

Misery stung Eleanor's eyes, but she forced herself to shove through the grief.

"I will, but there's something I've GOT to tell security, Ina. There's a man in the hospital who's only pretending to be a doctor. He's dangerous and he's been lying to everyone—"

Before she was even able to finish the sentence, medical alarms blared out. Within moments a team of grim-faced doctors and nurses were racing towards Cody's room.

CHAPTER 7

From Out
of the Pit

Something was following them through the trees.

Koemi felt as if she were running in a nightmare, that horrid sensation of sprinting as hard as you can but getting nowhere, as if your feet are mired in glue. Up ahead, Tsukiko's nightdress billowed, but it was as though Koemi were being taunted by the forest itself. However hard she tore through raking thickets that lashed her exposed skin like stinging whips, her mother never seemed to get any closer. Tsukiko remained always on the edge of visibility, vanishing entirely for heart-stopping seconds, then reappearing as a ghostly white flash half glimpsed through the mesh of branches.

With the canopy of trees pressing down like a black ceiling, Koemi felt as if she were running down an underground tunnel. Getting through the gloom was like struggling through the depths of a silt-choked lake. The forest floor flying beneath Koemi's feet might as well have been the surface of Pluto for all the detail she could make out, and she could only pray that her toes wouldn't snag on a treacherous creeper and throw her face-first into that impenetrable mulch of darkness and decay.

Throughout her young life, Koemi had lived in the vicinity of Aokigahara, but this was the first time she had ever felt genuine fear within its limits. Gradually, Koemi came to another horrible realization: it *hadn't* been just a fevered fantasy as she'd torn across those fields, there really was an awful *presence* keeping pace with her. Before, it had lived only in her imagination, as a mad, mocking cackle hidden in the rattle of the ambulance or a disgusting snicker beneath the laughter she'd used to save Moriko and Katsu. It was like a lurking, vile stench she could never quite identify or locate. Not anymore, though; now it was out in the open, thrashing through the undergrowth beside her, leaping like a tattered ghost through the inky air, bounding from bough to branch to bush.

As if the entity realized that she could now sense it, it began to focus on her. She felt its attention slither across her like icy nails trailing along her flesh. She wasn't going crazy. It wasn't all in her mind. This evil was real, and it hated her.

"Give up, Koemi. Tsukiko wants to die..."

Koemi let slip a whimper. It *spoke*. Openly, directly. The thing—the Whisperer—it had a voice that she heard through her own ears, not just as an echo inside her tortured mind.

"You can't save everyone... If you just let Tsukiko go, she can rest," hissed the malevolent spirit in a voice like cockroaches rustling over ashes.

"Think of how easy it would be to stop running. You're so young. You shouldn't have to deal with this. And you're in so much pain now..."

Koemi dry-swallowed. As vile as the voice was, it was

somehow seductive. Its logic was plausible and terribly, horribly persuasive. She *was* too young to have to deal with all this. She *should* have been playing hide-and-seek with girls and boys of her own age, not trying to catch her suicidal mother in a lightless hell forest. It would have been so much easier to sit down there and forget all about her desperate mission.

As if in the grip of a trance, Koemi began to sway and weave, exhaustion abruptly catching up with her.

"Why don't you sit down for a spell? A rest to gain your strength," the hissing voice offered slyly. *"You'll never be able to catch her anyway."*

Koemi's resolve was crumbling. Her footsteps faltered. She couldn't laugh; she could barely even cry anymore. If only she could think of something funny or joyful, an image, a song, a silly rhyme to access her healing laughter...

But no! Tsukiko had suddenly stopped! Her pale, wavering form was motionless for the first time since they'd entered the forest, twenty yards to Koemi's left. Koemi *could* catch up. The voice was lying! There was still hope...

Koemi shook her head to clear the feelings of horror the specter had conjured. Its words were like a cloud of filthy black flies sleeting onto her face, coating her cheeks and slipping down her throat. It made her feel sick just to have those thoughts in her mind, like an infection that ate away at the brain. Koemi returned her eyes to the path ahead. Her heart almost stopped. Tsukiko had vanished.

"Mother! It's me, it's Koemi! Where are you? PLEASE! Please answer me!" Koemi screamed between her gasping breaths as images of her mother's pale, lifeless face on the ambulance gurney flooded her mind. It took all the strength of body *and* soul for Koemi to keep on running and not crumple into a sobbing heap. Sensing Koemi's despair, the specter bounded up into a nearby tree and leaned over to hiss into her ear.

"Once upon a time there was a young mother who had the most beautiful three daughters and the most handsome, loving husband in the whole wide world. Do you want to know what happened next?"

Dread rose in Koemi's chest. She couldn't bear to hear what was coming next, and she put on another burst of speed. She reached the spot where Tsukiko had vanished, but didn't stop. Unable to check her momentum, she erupted through a wall of leaves and into a dingy glade carpeted by decaying moss. Koemi's stomach coiled with nausea as she saw ripples of movement writhing across the forest floor, bugs and other insects restlessly migrating in waves.

She immediately saw why her mother had appeared to vanish. Screened by the glade's perimeter of matted foliage, Tsukiko was now on her hands and knees at the center of the clearing. Her whole body was trembling beneath her tissue-thin nightdress as she moaned piteously to herself.

"One day not so long ago the young mother and her beautiful, devoted family went out for a drive in their shiny, new car. The weather was good at first, but then the rain came down, down, down," the monstrous presence narrated in a slippery, gleeful voice.

"The handsome, loving father was a very safe driver...but the man coming in the other direction wasn't—he was half drunk on sake! He took the curve far too late and careened across the road, skidding straight into the shiny, new car and smashing it clean off the road, where it slammed into an ancient black pine. The car was crushed on both sides! The handsome, loving father

and one of the beautiful daughters died instantly. The other two daughters survived—hooray! Screaming with grief, the young mother managed to drag the littlest daughter to safety. She was about to go back for her other child when, oh dear, the gas tank caught fire and the shiny car EXPLODED! Luckily, the drunk driver escaped without even a scratch!"

Koemi shuddered at the voice's ghastly, chatty rendition of her family's tragedy. It was obvious that while the vile spirit was definitely speaking out loud, only Koemi could hear its words. Her mother didn't react to the story at all. However, the Whisperer was still having an effect on her, accelerating her psychological disintegration as it radiated an invisible cloud of poisonous despair.

Suddenly, the Whisperer struck out in a new and even more horrible way. Without warning, Koemi was assaulted by a barrage of pictures stabbing directly into her mind, images of the crash, of flames and of blood, snapshots of the torn metal and the wet asphalt, the blank, empty eyes of her father and sweet sister, Rika. However much she fought, Koemi couldn't block out these images entirely, but she was able to resist their corrosive influence a little—however, these attacks were not directed at her alone.

Tsukiko's whole body jolted as if she'd been kicked. Then, muttering and crying, ignoring her daughter's desperate pleas, she started clawing at the ground with her fingernails! Horrified, Koemi instantly realized her mother was trying to dig a grave for herself with her own bare hands!

Koemi flew to her mother's side and tried to pry her away from the ghoulish task, but she simply didn't have the body mass to lever an adult up from the ground. Tsukiko continued to paw at the soil, her arms caked to the elbow in filth. Koemi begged her to stop; all the while the monstrous spirit flitted from tree to tree, bombarding them with ceaseless tales of tragedy and images of despair. Slowly it began to rain as well, heavier and heavier, faster and faster, so that the ground was quickly transformed into a seething mush. There was an abrupt crack of thunder, so loud it was like the sky had been torn in two, but no lightning came. No light, never any light.

"Mother! No! You mustn't! PLEASE!" Koemi shouted. Incredibly, Tsukiko's pallid face lashed round. Mother and daughter stared at each other for an agonizing, slow-burning moment. Koemi's heart leapt. She was certain she saw a flicker of sanity deep in the distraught woman's eyes.

Then the mulch of leaves and mud under Tsukiko's bloodied fingernails parted like a trapdoor and they both plummeted, screaming, into the unfathomable darkness beyond.

■ ■ ■ ■ ■

In the clinging blackness of the pit, Koemi thrashed about, searching for her mother. The sky was a ragged oval fifteen or twenty feet above them, only visible because it was a slightly paler shade of dark than the shadows all around. As she looked up, little landslides of pebbles showered her face. A cascade of muddy water ran into her eyes, half blinding her. Panic seized the young girl and she flailed around even more desperately. Her palm encountered something soft and trembling. Tsukiko moaned quietly, more in sorrow than in pain. Koemi gasped with relief.

Daughter and mother clung to each other, Koemi sobbing into Tsukiko's hair. She was intensely thankful finally to have coaxed a normal human response from Tsukiko, even if it had required them to be pitched headfirst into a hellish crack in the earth. It was a short-lived respite, however.

"*Think of all the horrors of this world,*" said the Whisperer, somehow hanging inches above them. It didn't have a body, mouth or lungs. It was the very floating embodiment of despair without flesh.

"*All the endless death and abuse and destruction,*" the thing continued in a lethal hiss. "*There's no hope. Innocents suffer in darkness everywhere, all over the globe. Wouldn't it be better just to give up and let humanity get on with tearing itself apart? Lie down in the mud and sleep in the comforting blanket of the dark, dreamless and soft. Sleep, Tsukiko... Sleep, Koemi...*"

Horrors began to rain down then, interspersed with the hammering, tiny fists of the rain, images of tragedies from a hundred lands burying them in an avalanche of despair: worshippers crushed in the collapse of a church; starving children, their bellies hugely swollen, too weak even to bat away the flies on their broken lips; the smoking wreck of a wedding party in the Middle East, struck by a bomb detonated nearby; a gleaming, red family Toyota slamming against a huge tree and exploding again and again into a column of cackling flames...

Koemi felt Tsukiko go slack under this onslaught, the last shreds of her willpower sluicing away like bathwater down the drain. Koemi pulled sharply at her mother but couldn't get a response. Tsukiko's eyes were dull like old rubber. In the belly of the earth and on the verge of losing everything, the little girl of the dancing laughter dived into the deepest reservoirs of her memories. She racked the mental closets of her earliest recollections for some tiny emotional handhold to hang on to.

"Papa's bow tie!" Koemi suddenly yelped.

Her voice was so weak she was certain she wouldn't be heard over the white noise of the storm, but no. Her words prompted an involuntary response from Tsukiko, a strangled squeak in the blackness. Not a squeak—a laugh in the middle of her tears! A frightened, utterly reflexive peep of humor, more a snivel than a snicker, but it was *humor* all the same.

What was more, when Tsukiko laughed, Koemi was sure she sensed the pressing darkness recoil just a little, as if in surprise. The Whisperer, their unyielding enemy, *flinched*.

"Mama! Mama! That's it, Papa's bow tie! Hold on to that— remember how he used to wear it even on the weekends, and how blue it was! So goofy, and silly, but so joyful! He knew it looked ridiculous, but it made us all laugh, so he wore it whenever he could!"

Koemi concentrated on an image of her father, Kenji, smiling down in a smartly pressed shirt, the neat segments of the bow tie like petals of a flower at his throat.

"Yes! I see it!" her mother exclaimed, and laughed again through her tears. "I'd try and get him to take it off when we went to meet my parents, but that just made him more determined! Oh, oh, and remember when he fitted it with a little motor on Kamiko's birthday but didn't tell anybody? He stood up at the height of the party with his tie spinning round and around. The whole place roared with hysterics!"

Bravely, Koemi dug deeper into her mother's memories of their lost family. She knew she had to break through that bitter shell of grief that encased their past like a cyst. Koemi had to help Tsukiko escape from this lethal cycle of misery. But how? She concentrated on the blue of Kenji's bow tie, that was the key, and—

Abruptly, she was somehow *inside* Tsukiko's memories.

She stood in the living room of their cozy Tokyo apartment. *Zabuton* cushions were arranged around the table, and Kenji, Kamiko and Rika were already there, cross-legged, laughing uproariously as they played a card game. This vision was a baffling, thrilling experience, but it gave Koemi hope that her mother *could* be saved from her own despair and the attacks of their enemy.

Tsukiko was there as well, but not her younger self. It was the bedraggled Tsukiko in a torn nightdress from the forest. She shied away from this cheerful domestic scene as if it were a pack of snarling wolves. Kenji beckoned, but Tsukiko shook her head and hid her face against the wall. Koemi gently pried her mother's palm free from her body and drew her towards the rest of the family. Tsukiko fought her at every step, but eventually they both sat to join the game. Koemi felt a tiny release somewhere in the ether, like a key turning in a lock. She smiled. Tsukiko did too, very tentatively. Kamiko and Rika grinned. Kenji's eyes creased as humor crinkled all over his face, and he touched his bow tie. Amazingly, it began to spin...

Papa's bow tie was so blue it positively glowed, radiating soft waves of sapphire-colored light. Koemi opened her eyes and the memories folded neatly back into her mother's mind. In the forest, still in the pit, a warm, blue glow was leaking out around Koemi and Tsukiko. It unraveled into washes of different hues—aquamarine, turquoise, azure, teal—as it dissolved the shadows. It was her father's light, and it spread out through their bodies in the same way Koemi channelled life force energy to save Katsu and Moriko. Only *this* light was from the memory of the bow tie!

Koemi clapped her palms together with delight. Her

mother's eyes were still firmly closed, but she laughed also, nervously but quite naturally. Soon they were both laughing together, shakily at first but then with increasing power. Their defiant humor didn't go unnoticed.

The Whisperer's anger felt like a horrible thickening of the air, a vast, stinging pressure in Koemi's inner ear. The slippery voice sneered and mocked and shouted and raged. The torrent of awful images redoubled, becoming a positive tsunami of horrors. For long seconds Koemi was certain they would fail and collapse back into the soil to die.

But then their laughter began to blend together, synchronizing as it braided into one almost melodic sound. This sound seemed to feed the blue light that in turn strengthened their rejoicing in a self-fulfilling loop. Soon their joy became a bright, irresistible force fighting against the press of writhing shadows, pushing, pushing—

Until finally it broke through the darkness like a matted, stinking dam of fallen leaves that had gummed up the pure flow of a sparkling stream. The Whisperer fled. Koemi could hear it racing away through the trees in incoherent fury, smashing through the undergrowth.

Koemi and Tsukiko were alone. They were safe, but they didn't stop laughing. It kept on rising out of them in happy swells, up towards the branches and the dim sky far above. The storm had broken, and starlight was trickling down into the pit. Tsukiko turned to her daughter, her face gleaming softly, and she smiled, all the muscles of her cheeks relaxing fully for the first time in weeks.

"I've been so wrong, my daughter," she said in a voice that was weary but resolute. "It *is* good to be alive."

■ ■ ■ ■ ■

Koemi couldn't stop grinning as they trudged back through the cheerfully rustling forest. She kept glancing over her shoulder at Tsukiko. Her mother's nightdress might have been ruined, her exposed skin streaked with trails of mud and dirt, but to Koemi's eyes she glowed with life.

The loss of Kenji, Kamiko and Rika was not lessened, but it was no longer a wound that her soul had to constantly drain out into the world. Finally, Tsukiko was able to experience what Koemi had felt since the terrible day of the accident: the peace of knowing that her family was not lost but surrounded her forever with their love. Koemi would never have to worry about leaving her mother alone with her grief again.

Finding their way back to the more well-travelled paths after the ordeal of the pit wasn't much of a chore and, anyway, there was no need to hurry. Dawn would soon be diluting the night with its milky luster. Eventually, they broke the tree line and stepped out into the fields beyond. An owl hooted back in the ragged throng of boughs, as if bidding them farewell. Instinctively, Koemi glanced backwards, and to her astonishment, she saw an old man leaning against a red maple tree.

The man was hunched over with extreme age, his face so wrinkled and ancient that it resembled a cross between a knuckle and a gargoyle. He was dressed in ordinary gray sweatpants and a blue hooded top, but, impossibly, he seemed bathed in a sourceless golden light, his wisps of white hair stirring in a breeze that simply wasn't there. It was as if he were standing in a warm summer's day while they were still deep in the early morning gloom, despite there being less than ten feet between them.

Koemi's eyes met the man's cataract-cloudy gaze, and he frowned at her, his expression grave. Tsukiko, however, was totally oblivious to the newcomer's presence, exactly as she had been of the Whisperer's existence. Did Koemi's abilities mean that she was privy to a hidden world that the rest of the populace was unable to detect? This thought made her suddenly frightened again, and she felt horribly lonely with that burden. The Whisperer was gone. It had only been defeated, *not* destroyed. Would it return? And if it did, would she be able to fight it off again on her own?

Koemi suddenly heard a heavily accented voice echoing in her mind—the old man's voice? She couldn't tell, and his motionless lips didn't let slip any clues.

"*Soon,*" the voice said. "*Not yet...but soon.*"

CHAPTER 8

Break Free!

Harata knew that time was running out as her paws splashed desperately through the puddles and the rain smashed down in blazing sheets all around her. The monsoon was so heavy that it felt like the end of the world out there on the mosaic of Lahore's rooftops. She was horribly aware of Spotty's heart like a frenzied *dholak* drum in his chest, pitter-pattering frantically as she nudged him along the ledge over another dizzying drop. The rain was making Tahir's scent all but impossible to track, so she'd urged Spotty up onto the narrow maze of walkways high above the congested lanes, hoping that they might spot him.

The personal ad she'd found had named Tahir's target as a physician from the Shia religious minority. He worked at the nearby Mayo hospital. Mayo was a massive institution not far from the Walled City, situated between Anarkali and Gawal-mandi. Tahir couldn't just stroll in there and find the doctor, but the ad had listed a stall on nearby Food Street where the man went to buy pastries every day! If Harata could intercept

Tahir en route there was the possibility she could inhabit a dog and steal Tahir's bag, or use Spotty to distract him, or even hinder him somehow with her astral form. That was the theory, anyway, but Tahir already had a formidable head start, and now there was the relentless rain to contend with.

Shrieks of delight darted up from the street as a group of teenage girls in hijabs under a half-broken umbrella were suddenly splashed by a passing taxi. Car horns honked out in a chorus on the main road while one enterprising soul stood on the corner, hawking cheap plastic coats from a hemp bag, joking with the pedestrians still braving the deluge.

Spotty mewed miserably as he slunk along one sopping wall, trying to find shelter under a rare sloping eave. His fur was plastered to his back in slick clumps, and his tail curled up like a stiff antenna in mute resentment. The power of the rain was so great that it obscured the view in every direction. Lahore had become a blurry watercolor, all fuzzy, pale oblongs and abstract towers of gray glass. Realizing that their rooftop hunt was futile, Harata persuaded her furry surrogate to leap back down to the alleyway.

Spotty landed heavily in yet another puddle and yowled pitiably. Harata could feel the frustration radiating through his little feline mind, and it cut at her to the quick, but she *had* to find Tahir before... She didn't want to think what might happen.

She abruptly felt Spotty go rigid as his senses prickled. He froze and stared intently towards the mouth of the alleyway, his ears standing at attention. A blurry group of shadows, half obscured by the driving downpour, had blocked off the light. Spotty's animal instincts kicked in. He bared his fangs, hissing like a broken gas main, and carefully began to retreat, his gaze never leaving the sinister, advancing shades.

Suddenly Harata and Spotty both heard a bass growl emerge from behind them. Spotty's head whipped round and Harata witnessed a towering, black shape emerging through the curtains of a dirty waterfall cascading from an overflowing drain. Harata felt Spotty's body tremble from nose tip to tail with dread.

The bullmastiff pawed the ground, water dripping off its heaving black flanks, steam curling like smoke around its massive jaws. Harata heard cruel mocking laughter ring out inside her mind as the dog bounded towards the defenseless cat...

■ ■ ■ ■ ■

The moment she had realized what insanity Tahir was involved in, Harata had run straight to Kedar.

"Father, don't say a word, just listen to your daughter for once," she blurted in a fearless rush as Kedar's face grew dark. "Papa, we have to follow Tahir right now. He's got himself in terrible, terrible trouble. He's fallen in with the same group of Wahhabist extremists responsible for the High Court killings! He's off RIGHT NOW to Mayo hospital to kill innocent Shia doctors—"

Heaving with emotion, she thrust the paper with its desperate scrawling directly under Kedar's bulbous nose.

Kedar didn't say a word. Harata stared at his furrowed forehead, willing him to understand the gravity of the situation. Didn't he realize his son's life dangled in the balance? If

Kedar had had any affinity for the vibrations of the universe, he would certainly have been able to feel Tahir's peril…

Kedar frowned slowly. He peered closer at the ratty news-sheet she proffered, then surged up from his chair and grabbed Harata painfully by the wrist

"No! NO! Father, innocent people will DIE!" Harata shrieked at the top of her voice, but she was irresistibly wrenched from the room by Kedar's adult strength. Her brothers came and stood open-mouthed in the doorways. Syed stepped forward with a worried expression, but Rafiq pulled him back.

It was no use. Kedar just tore open her bedroom and pro-pelled her inside with all his might.

"And there you shall stay until you can learn proper obe-dience!" Kedar roared through the wooden barrier. "What's more, if you slander Tahir's honor and my parenting once more, on the memory of your poor, kind mother, so help me Allah, I shall beat you within an inch of your life!"

Harata swung back in her room, tearing at her hair, mind whirring with possible schemes and solutions and miraculous escape routes. There was only one: her powers, which she barely understood and trusted even less. There was no other option. Harata bolted for the window.

"Spotty! Spo-o-otty!" she sung. If she just used her spirit flight, her perspective would be far too lofty to pinpoint her brother in the teeming streets. She needed the help of a born hunter.

Within moments she caught a flicker of dark motion, and a little tabby face bobbed above her sill. She fed Spotty scraps of yesterday's dinner, and he purred through his eager munching. Harata's stomach clenched.

"You're such a good friend," she told the cat in a soft tone, scratching him behind the ears. "But I'm so sorry, we don't have any time."

She tugged free of her body and slid into the warm crevice of Spotty's mind.

■ ■ ■ ■ ■

The jaws of the bullmastiff loomed like a cave full of stalactites.

Every cell in Spotty's tiny body screamed at him to leap *away* from this monster, but Harata knew the beast would catch the cat within a matter of paces and rip him to shreds. Instead, hating herself for using her powers this way, she rammed a mental suggestion like a glittering spike deep into her pet's mind.

Spotty ran *towards* the bullmastiff and between the stinking arch of the dog's front legs, beneath his ragged belly, then out again under his foul tail!

There was no way these half-insane beasts could have anticipated such a sophisticated human feign, thought Harata as she goaded Spotty towards the nearest drainpipe and freedom—where, to her horror, she found a drooling rottweiler already waiting! This time, Harata simply had to rely on Spotty's feline agility to save them. The rottweiler's jaws pistoned towards the cat, but Spotty's spine flicked like an eel and the hound's teeth snapped on thin air. Spotty streaked away up the drain like a flash of furry lightning.

The dogs had *known* Spotty might have run between their leader's legs. They had reasoned it out in a cold and calculating fashion. There was nothing normal about these creatures.

They didn't bark, or whine, or deviate from their prey. Moving as one they surged after Spotty like heat-seeking missiles, the only sounds in the alleyway were the hot gusts of their breath and the skittering of their claws on the brickwork, up after Harata and Spotty.

Their eyes weren't bloodshot, Harata saw now, but throbbed inside with a callous, scarlet light. These animals weren't merely stray dogs driven mad by parasites. Impossibly, they *knew* Spotty had a spirit passenger, or *something* inside them knew she was there—a dark, controlling intelligence.

Suddenly it struck the girl, as Spotty negotiated the treacherous roof brimming with rain—did she have a nemesis? Was there another person with the same powers as her but an opposing impulse towards destruction? There was no time to follow this awful train of reasoning, though. Harata might not have been vulnerable in spirit form (as far as she knew!), but Spotty remained in direst peril. She simply couldn't live with herself if she left Spotty to die, torn apart by these hellhounds. If she abandoned her poor pet now, she wouldn't be the person Syed and her friends loved, nor true to the memory of her noble mother.

Still, even as she drove Spotty to leap across a yawning gap, she knew Tahir would be making his final approach now. She imagined…

Tahir trudged hesitantly along Food Street, his breath wheezing tight with asthma, head down low as he muttered broken snatches of prayers to try to calm himself.

Spotty landed short and scrabbled desperately to pull himself to safety. The animal's panic roared in Harata's mind as she felt the slippery surface skate woozily beneath her frantic paws. Overhead, to their horror, all the dogs flew easily over the gap and landed safely with a thump—except for the rotweiller, who miscalculated his jump and slid back too fast, unable to check his momentum. Harata caught a fleeting glimpse of the animal's mad, rolling eyes before he disappeared over the edge. He fell without making a sound.

Tahir's palms were slick with sweat. He was shivering from the rain running down the back of his collar and worried that he might throw up. It was like his whole body were rebelling against his appalling mission.

Spotty managed—just—to lever himself up onto the roof, only to be confronted by a bristling storm of teeth and claws and sickness. Spotty dodged and darted in between legs, around tails, spinning away from the jaws of doom, whirling like a tiny tornado of fear, filthy rainwater splashing in every direction. If he stopped moving, Harata silently shouted at Spotty, he was done for.

On Food Street, Tahir fiddled with the clasp on his tote bag. He gripped the gun's butt. Could he do this? Could he kill another human being in cold blood? His footsteps faltered as his thoughts did. Then he spotted the fateful pastry stall and the Shia doctor just standing there.

Yes, he could do it.

Spotty suddenly jerked to a halt so hard his vision blurred. He fought wildly for a few heartbeats, yowling, not under-standing the impediment until he flicked a look behind him and saw that the bullmastiff had Spotty's tail between his teeth!

Before either Harata or Spotty could react, the beast shook his massive head, dashing Spotty violently against the roof. Agony lanced Spotty's body, the sensations exploding like sun-spots in Harata's mind. His pain couldn't hurt her physically, but it was still a terrible shock. Everything she experienced through another creature's sharp senses was uncommonly vivid, even pain, and she wouldn't have it any other way—it kept her from ever forgetting the fragile nature of life.

"Eyes!" Harata screamed in Spotty's brain. Like a jack-in-the-box bursting open, Spotty's claws caught the bullmastiff by surprise, raking his shining, blood-colored eyes, making them actually bleed. For the very first time since the assault began, one of the dogs made a sound—the bullmastiff howled in rage, which, of course, allowed Spotty's ruined tail to slip through his fangs.

Tahir centered himself. A terrible calm had come over him. "This is God's will," he whispered to himself. He walked towards the brightly colored stall, clouds of fragrant cooking smoke flaring out into the moist air. The doctor was oblivious to Tahir's approach, guffawing with four of his colleagues, not a care in the world. Tahir would shoot them all, he decided grimly.

Spotty limped towards one of the roof's exits, but his way was nimbly blocked by one of the dogs. Soon every avenue was covered. In shivering terror, Spotty retreated towards a sheer drop while the dogs crowded slowly around him, confident that their prey was finally cornered. In desperation, Spotty turned to look over the edge, mewing plaintively for an escape route that didn't exist. There was no way he could make the jump to the nearest building. The pack had him trapped.

"Have faith, little one," Harata whispered in his mind. "Leap!"

A beat of instinctive hesitation, then she felt Spotty's muscles tense and uncoil—followed by the thrilling peace of falling. Half blinded and raging, the bullmastiff instantly followed, only realizing a moment too late where Spotty's leap was aimed. They plummeted off the roof and arced out into empty space.

Tahir's breath was quick inside his throat as he darted through the crowd, bumping people aside, his gaze pinned on his target.

Spotty landed perfectly on the precarious, tiny lip of the apartment building opposite, his momentum carrying him head over paws like a furry bowling ball, rolling him through the narrow entrance of the broken air vent Harata had noticed when they first made their leap to the building above. Inside was a snug metal box, an impregnable den for Spotty to hide in. The vent was awkward and barely accessible. The jump would be virtual suicide for the larger dogs, and anyway, their snouts would barely fit inside the mouth of the vent.

Behind Spotty, the bullmastiff rebounded off the wall above the vent and dropped out of sight, howling.

Tahir's hand closed on the gun in his bag. His palm was dry now. He was ready. His forefinger curled around the trigger.

"No!" Harata moaned in her bedroom. Spotty was safe, but Tahir was surely doomed. "My brother," Harata whispered. "I've failed you…"

In desperation she launched her spirit body away from Spotty as forcefully as she could, a vivid picture of Tahir's face burned into her consciousness. To her amazement she found that image of her brother worked like a mental anchor, and she was tugged straight towards him. Harata rocketed through the city faster than she had ever moved before, faces, signs, buildings smearing into rays of blurry color as they passed.

Then she was there, hovering behind Tahir, the rain slanting through her invisible body—

But it was still too late! Tahir was drawing his pistol *right now,* though none of the people huddling under the kiosk awnings had noticed yet. Time seemed to stutter like frames of celluloid catching in a faulty film projector.

There was only one last thing Harata could try, something she'd cringed away from ever since she had discovered her powers. She launched herself into Tahir's mind.

▪ ▪ ▪ ▪ ▪

Tahir's consciousness was a terrible place of turbulent, red skies and black sand clawed by flashes of scarlet lightning. Harata and her brother stood facing each other on a street very much like Food Street but populated by crowds of black-robed figures with hideously deformed wooden masks instead of faces. They dashed past but never looked her in the eye.

"Harata?" Tahir gaped at her in astonishment. "Where are we? I...I was just on Food Street, I was going to—"

"You still *are* there, Tahir. You're still on that street and I know what you were about to do. This is the space inside your mind, where your true emotions live. We are frozen in the moment *before* you do that terrible deed and destroy your life."

In his mind, Tahir stared at her. This close to his soul, Harata could sense the generous, happy boy he used to be. That man still existed inside Tahir despite the horrors of his internal landscape.

"Tahir, people must change their beliefs to change their lives," she implored, sending waves of love rippling towards him. They appeared like a column of beautiful, swirling, blue petals. "We are all interconnected on the deepest level, Tahir. We're one!"

Tahir scowled, shaking his head like a stubborn child.

"Lies!" he shouted, but Harata could sense he wanted to surrender to love. The red darkness in his mind was drawing back like a slow-motion tide. Harata pushed her advantage.

"You must access the unseen dimension of life to find where you belong, Tahir. Focus on that which lies beyond the material world.. You will understand your connection to others deep in your veins and be able to expand your vision to include a larger awareness. Then—and *only* then—you will find the power you seek flowing naturally around you. There's a life force that guides you at all times. It flows through your bones, your brain, your soul. You hold the universe in every cell of your body!"

Tahir's eyes were open again, and he was staring at her. He marvelled at the whirl of petals that now surrounded him like a protective shield. Hopeful curiosity was eating away at his emotional battlements.

"You know this is wrong, don't you?" Harata continued. "To do what you are about to do? All life is precious. Tahir, even though you don't know it, your life has a grand purpose on this planet. On a deeper level of awareness, you know why you are here, but you must find that purpose for yourself—not be drawn away from the path by these false prophets of violence and prejudice. Will you be on the side of destroyers or healers, Tahir?"

"I...I don't know," whispered Tahir. "Who are you?" he demanded. "Are you real?"

"I'm your—" Harata almost admitted that she was his sister come to aid him, but then her caution pulled her up short as she thought of the dogs and her nemesis. It might not be safe for either of them if Tahir knew her secret. She opted to garnish the truth just a little.

"I am your conscience and your angel, Tahir. I am with you

always, and I love you from the roots of your being. You are surrounded by Universal Love. There is nothing left to fear..."

Tahir's inner self nodded, tracks of tears gleaming on his cheeks. His expression suddenly yielded in remorse.

"Yes," he breathed, and the sun broke through the burgundy clouds above, flooding his mind with a pure, steady light. The masks fell off the hunched, scuttling creatures to reveal beautiful human faces, which turned up towards the sky in smiling expectation.

Harata relaxed, and the vision of Tahir's consciousness drained away like water, leaving them both back in the physical world on Food Street. Tahir was no longer aware of Harata's intangible presence, and he blinked in confusion. A beat later he hurriedly stowed the gun back in his bag before any passersby noticed.

The Shia doctor hurried past with one of his young colleagues. He smiled at the dumbstruck Tahir and offered him a friendly little salute, which her brother echoed automatically with a stunned expression. Harata grinned invisibly.

■ ■ ■ ■ ■

The rain had stopped, as if someone had twisted off a hose tap. Colorfully dressed Lahoris were emerging from under awnings and other impromptu shelters, jovial and shaking droplets from the hems of their silk shawls or wringing out their *kameez* tunic sleeves. A happy solidarity reigned amongst these ordinary people driven into unexpected companionship with strangers, united by something larger than themselves. This cloud of cheerfulness wafted up towards Harata. She was delighted that Tahir was safe, and Spotty. These sectarian attacks were a blight upon the honor of Pakistan, but she *could* use her powers to foil them and to save lives after all.

Afterwards, Harata stayed with Tahir to make sure his repentance held, flying close above him as he stumbled down to the river, where he tossed the tote bag into the water. He walked back home and went straight to Kedar's den.

"Father, I almost did a terrible, terrible thing today," he told their papa. He went on to confess all, and he asked for his father's help and forgiveness. Kedar was a hard, often self-involved man, but he truly loved his family and, as Harata had hoped, this moment softened both men's hearts. She knew as they embraced, that in time, this would actually bring the whole family together.

With a contented spectral sigh, Harata drifted happily out through the wall and into the sky. One dark cloud remained, though: her nemesis and the helldogs.

For the rest of the afternoon she swept the city for clues, but there was no sign of the dogs or the malevolent intelligence that inhabited them, so Harata finally floated back to the original alley where the battle had begun. Her joy was lifted again as she witnessed Spotty sneaking out from his hiding place and leaping away with a flick of his (newly) crooked tail. Then she spotted a wizened, old man leaning against the alley wall. He wore incongruous Western clothes and was staring up at the sky. Was THIS her nemesis?

Suddenly, the man pointed at the exact spot where Harata's awareness hung, his eyes glittering with a frightening intensity.

He could see her!

Harata snapped back to her body, jackknifed up from the reed mat on the floor, and screamed.

CHAPTER 9

The Light
of Truth

L ogan had vanished.
 Immediately after Eleanor relayed her story to hospital
security, the whole hospital went into emergency lockdown.
While those in charge were scrupulously careful not to spread
any unnecessary alarm, security personnel—soon joined by
NYPD officers—were posted at every access point and anyone
passing in or out of the building was methodically checked.
They were given body searches, their possessions meticulously
examined, and their identities checked against a raft of police
databases.

Yet still—*somehow*—Logan managed to elude them.

It was as if he had simply sprouted wings and flown away.
The hospital authorities were as baffled as they were unnerved
by his Houdini impression, especially when it became clear
that he had effortlessly posed as a member of the staff for
weeks, coming and going as he pleased. Still, they continued
to rush around, checking doors and giving the impression
of furious, dedicated activity to ensure nothing like this ever
happened again. What else could they do?

None of this mattered to Ellie and her friends. All they could think of was Cody, and how he was dying, there, then, that evening.

■ ■ ■ ■ ■

While controlled chaos ruled in the corridor outside, Ellie, Frank, Spencer, Tammy and Lisa stood around Cody's bed, watching his chest jerk raggedly up and down in the low lamplight. His breath rasped muddily inside the cowl of his ventilator and, with the coils of plastic tubing that surrounded him, he looked like he was trapped in a high-tech briar patch. Cody's father had been contacted, but he was on a business trip to Detroit. He was struggling desperately to get back, but it didn't seem likely he'd arrive before morning and, by then, it would be too late. Cody's mom had died when he was a baby, also of cancer, so it was left to his friends to stand vigil over him and bear witness to his final moments.

Nobody said very much. Tammy wept while Lisa comforted her. Spencer stood very stiffly, clasping and unclasping his hands at his sides like he didn't know what to do with his body. Frank seemed the most at ease. He was desperately sad but radiated a calm acceptance, which they all appreciated. Eleanor stood apart from the others, hugging herself. This was all her fault.

Green auras *grew* cancer. That was what she'd worked out in the wake of Logan's unmasking, and it made a horrible kind of sense. Green really was the color of life, of flowering, of *expansion*. Of course all the patients she treated with green were full of energy—at first. Logan—if that was even his real name—had manipulated her into employing the color that would cause the most harm for every condition she treated. By far the worst outcome was with Cody, though. Using her auric power to focus the green light, she had actually *nourished* his tumors, not starved them. It was what had killed the pigeons, the first creatures she had killed. Logan had known the techniques he was teaching her were lethal. He'd planned it that way.

The more she dug into her recollections of their *friendship*, the more the awful, hidden logic started to slot together. The clues were all there; she had just been too naive to see them. Now she had time to pick apart the damning details. She remembered how Logan had never actually introduced her to any of his supposed patients—he'd just shown up in their rooms with Eleanor by his side. Everyone knew Ellie for her art and welcomed her warmly. That was what Logan had been relying on. But *why?* Why go to all those lengths to undermine her...unless she really was that important? Well, if that were the case, then how had she been fooled so easily, and why couldn't she save her friend?

Eleanor forced herself to gaze at Cody's aura, though it made her flinch with shame. His life force was virtually transparent now, cocooned by gluey stripes of white, leeching the color out of him. She halfheartedly tried to pull at the killing worms, disguising the action as fixing her hair clasp, but the deadly strands resisted, as they had done every time she'd attempted this since Cody fell into his coma. Ellie turned to Lisa, her eyes brimming.

"You saw it," she whispered to her plainspoken friend. "Logan's strange aura, how flat it seemed, you noticed straight away... If only I'd talked to you earlier, then—"

"You can't blame yourself. It wasn't your fault," Lisa

admonished kindly. "Logan did everything he could to convince you he was your guide. He set out to infiltrate this hospital with only one goal in mind: to discredit you so you could never teach the world and we would ALL lose the hope you offer! You can't let him win by blaming yourself."

"I love Cody…but he could NEVER keep a secret!" Spencer abruptly blurted into the silence, looking a little guilty, but everybody just laughed before fondly agreeing. Despite the sadness of the moment, this seemed to break the ice and warm the atmosphere.

"He loved to talk," Spencer continued, then a shadow passed over his face. "*Loves* to talk," he corrected himself. "Friends with everyone, always going up to new people, adopting all the waifs and strays."

Ellie smiled warmly, recalling how Cody had adopted her on that first fateful morning.

"He had the most infectious smile," murmured Tammy. "He could always get you to join in, even at the worst times."

"Remember when we all started making fun of Nurse Billy trying to help that old guy out of the slippery wheelchair? That was Cody's fault!"

"He was the best at cheering us up—I wish he could do that now," Frank admitted. "He was always the cheerleader. 'Everybody join in.' That should have been his catchphrase!"

"That's it!" Eleanor shrieked, and four sets of eyes instantly converged on her. For once she didn't feel self-conscious. She was simply electrified with sudden hope.

"I can't heal Cody," she told them. "Not *by myself*, but what if we ALL do it together?"

Clever Tammy was frowning, though, as she quickly spotted a flaw in the plan.

"How can we work together when half of us can't even see the auras properly!"

This was a perfectly valid point. Eleanor racked her brains for an answer. Then her eyes fell on her backpack propped up against Cody's chair, and the solution jumped up and slapped her.

"Where's the biggest piece of paper we can find in this hospital?" she demanded.

■ ■ ■ ■ ■

They borrowed a big, flapping sheet of paper from one of Saint Rafael's basement lecture halls and managed to smuggle it back to Cody's room. Even with a pad of that size, it was difficult for all five children to crowd around without elbow nudges and barging, but they managed it somehow. They worked in a feverish hush. Ellie naturally took charge, but as the picture developed she could feel all their different energies braiding together, working in harmony.

Working with bright pastels, each child had a different spectrum of color to concentrate on, and exactly as Eleanor had before them, her friends were able to move their fingertips from the page to the air, brushing confidently at the yellows, oranges and aquamarines buried in Cody's corona beneath the rapacious white snakes. Eleanor was able to shape the whole process with minute tweaks and squeezes. Healing in this way was nothing like her previous efforts. They were weaving a tapestry of petals together, stitching and folding translucent rainbow arcs around the thrashing pit of white serpents.

Still, it was an enormous effort, and soon sweat was pouring off their faces. More than once Cody stiffened as if in distress, or trembled like a leaf in a storm. Slowly but surely, though, they were coaxing their friend back from the lip of death!

"Yes!" shouted Eleanor. "It's happening! Careful now, all together, just there—"

A barrage of bleeps erupted out of the monitor beside Cody's head. Quick-thinking Frank leapt across the room hit the reset button to quiet the machine before a staff member could investigate. Just then the white worms surged unexpectedly. Instantly, the kids retaliated, which caused an explosion of colors to blaze out from Cody's body of light. It seemed to blind all their auric visions for a moment, and no one knew what was going on.

"Didn't it work?" asked Lisa, her voice quivering with uncertainty.

"No...no, he's gone," sobbed Spencer in a strangled voice. The others all bowed their heads or squeezed their eyes closed in anguish.

Then, Tammy said dryly, "No, he isn't—his eyes are open!"

It was true. Cody's eyes *were* open and full of bright life!

"Spence!" everybody roared at the mortified lad, but it was a happy outburst. Cody was fine. He gestured to his ventilator with a querying look.

"His mask!" exclaimed Lisa. "Let's get that thing off him! Quick!"

Spencer almost went head over heels as he sprinted off to find Nurse Ina.

▦ ▦ ▪ ▦ ▦

Much later, Eleanor sat on a hard, plastic bench, kicking her feet idly back and forth as she waited for Rachel to finish her shift. Above her a skylight rattled as it bore the brunt of the downpour outside, rain lashing the glass like a hail of needles. She knew Rachel wouldn't have remembered her umbrella despite the dire warnings on the morning weather report. She never did.

Eleanor was parked in a deserted corridor on the far side of Saint Rafael's, away from the kids' ward. To be honest, this suited her mood. Despite all the day's excitement she had reverted to her introverted nature and needed time by herself to process all the overwhelming developments.

In the aftermath of their intervention, Cody's condition had improved exponentially. All of his attending doctors came running, but they were utterly at a loss to explain his miraculous recovery. Someone ran to call Cody's dad, to give him the joyful news. Among all the shrugging and head-scratching adults, the kids shared secret smiles. Eleanor and her friends had decided to keep their auric abilities to themselves—for the time being, at least. After all, who knew what other enemies Eleanor might have out there, and what they might be capable of?

Ellie peered down at her lap and the beautiful plaque of polished teak she was holding. It was bizarre how such a truly horrendous day could end with so many pieces of good news all at once. The plaque read, in swirly, calligraphic script, "Presented to Eleanor Henning, age eight, Spring 2004, for exceptional achievements in the fields of painting and drawing."

It was the national art competition her mom had entered

her in all those weeks ago—the Golden Wings Scholarship. She'd won first prize. Rachel had hung on to the check that accompanied the award. It was a shockingly large amount and would make a great nest egg for Ellie's college fund.

The rain pelted with redoubled power against the skylight, and a flash of lightning suddenly burnt the corridor into a photo-negative image of itself. Ellie shifted apprehensively on the bench; for some reason she suddenly felt...uneasy. Was it just the storm? She looked up. A figure was standing at the other end of the corridor, watching her.

Logan.

Thunder crashed outside, and the lights went out! The building's generator had blown. Ellie jammed her knuckles in her mouth to prevent herself from screaming.

Had he seen her before the lights went out?

As quietly as she could, she stepped out of her sneakers and stood. Her stockinged feet made no sound on the gleaming floor. Awfully, Logan was blocking the route back to the more populated areas of the building. If she called out for help, he would catch her long before anybody could come to her aid. Eleanor began to inch towards the far end of the corridor. That way led to the secretarial offices and administrative records. She'd never been so scared in her life.

"Ellieeeeee?" a voice slithered out behind her. She turned automatically just as the next lightning flash blazed the scene into a monochromatic frieze.

Logan was coming after her, taking his time, grinning. She only caught an instant's glimpse of him, but she was sure there was something wrong with his skin. His whole face seemed to be bubbling like molten metal, his shoulders twisted by some bizarre mutation. His aura was a jagged thing of thrashing, black spikes. He looked, quite simply, like a monster.

Ellie *ran*.

Behind her, she heard dark laughter.

■ ■ ■ ■ ■

Eleanor was hiding in the records room.

She had raced through a seemingly endless succession of identical unlit hallways, pursued by the monstrous Logan. The records room had been locked, but she knew which office the key was kept in. Within seconds, she raced into the sanctuary of the cold, cramped room and locked herself inside. The space was full of ceiling-high filing racks divided into narrow aisles. Eleanor retreated to the farthest, darkest corner, safe in the knowledge that while she might have been locked in, at least she was safe. Rachel would soon raise the alarm and help would come running. Then she heard the door unlock…and heavy footsteps creep inside the room.

So they both began a terrifying game of cat and mouse around the shadowy filing rows. Logan was as stealthy as a cat but, as terrified as she was, Ellie, the mouse, found that she did have an advantage. Her auric sight worked *through* the aisles. She could see Logan's approach by the glare of his inhuman aura around each corner.

In this manner, Ellie managed to keep ahead of her nemesis in the maze. But she could sense the air clotting with the growing rage and frustration of the thing that hunted her. Finally, after several long, desperate minutes, just as she thought her horrified heart might burst, she heard the soft clunk of the outer door closing and the clump of steps moving away. Eleanor didn't dare allow herself a sigh of relief, but still she walked silently towards the door.

"No," whispered a heavily accented voice in her ear—a man's voice, possibly Italian. "Don't go that way, it is a trap. The Corrupter is waiting."

Eleanor's head came around fast as she searched for the speaker, who must have been close by. But to her astonishment, she was still alone. Her eyes darted to a nearby air conditioning grill. Could the speaker have been in the vent system?

"Who's there? Who are you?" she hissed.

"I am your guide."

"I...I don't believe you. Show yourself."

"I cannot do that. But I will prove my insight. The Corrupter can hide his aura. He has realized that this is how you were tracking him. He has masked his energy field and waits outside the door."

Eleanor gnawed her lip in the dark. This made sense, but how could she trust a disembodied voice?

"I want to trust you, but... Won't you at least tell me your name to put my mind at ease?" she implored.

"We shall make a deal then, you and I. If you follow my instructions to the letter AND make it out alive, *then* I will tell you my name. How does that sound, Little Miss?"

Eleanor swallowed and nodded. A moment passed in silence, then she blurted quickly, "I'm sorry, yes! Yes, I'll take your hel—"

"I saw you nod," the voice commented.

But *how?* Eleanor marvelled. There was no time to mull over this enigma, however—the voice was barking out.

"Don't dither. Quickly, in the corner—above the ladder, see—the broken ceiling tile!"

Ellie's heart leapt. The voice wasn't lying. There were some stepladders and up above, hidden by the gloom, a broken ceiling panel! But she had to move—already the door lock was turning. She heard Logan curse in a barely human growl.

In a blink, she was at the steps and up them, pulling herself into the dusty void above the room. She was just in the nick of time, though, as she heard Logan—or the thing he was turning into—crash back into the room. He went raging like a force of nature along the aisles. Pure animal fear gripped her as she realized he was only feet below her.

"You can't stop. He'll be after you in a second. Come on, *crawl!*"

So she did, moving through the dark, the voice her constant guide. She navigated the spaces above the offices until suddenly the voice halted her.

"The electricity will come back on in a moment."

"How can you possibly know—" Ellie began.

"You haven't got any time," the voice thundered in her ear. "We need to drive him off. There's an emergency alarm on the far wall provided for maintenance crews working up here—"

Ellie found the Day-Glo yellow box and, just as she felt the throb of the generator coming back online, she slammed the rubberized alarm switch. Its siren wailed out below. This racket would obviously bring security running in seconds. To her horror, Eleanor heard the sheer uncontrollable rage of the thing Logan had become. It was a psychic roar that made the hairs all the way along her spine stand on end. She shivered, even though the sensation only lasted a matter of moments before snapping off abruptly.

"He is gone," concluded the voice with a hint of bitter satisfaction.

"How could you possibly have known he was able to

control his own aura like that?" Eleanor demanded of the darkness around her.

"I've been fighting the Corrupter so long I've learned a good many of his tricks without him even realizing I was doing it. Arrogance will ultimately be his downfall... Come on, I'm up on the roof where you used to meet him. Don't fret. It's quite safe now."

■ ■ ■ ■ ■

Eleanor raced out onto the rooftop. To her astonishment, her savior turned out to be an elderly, toothless, putty-faced man in stained jogging pants leaning against one of the air-conditioning stacks. He regarded her indifferently.

"You!" she exploded, unable to think of anything else to say. That was when she realized that the man was *sparkling*, like he was standing in a shaft of magical sunlight that illuminated him alone, only there was no source of light. It was the middle of the night.

The man didn't say anything, just scowled at her as if she'd interrupted his midmorning coffee and cookies. Instinctively, though, she did trust him. Logan had seemed utterly sincere on the surface, but in reality, he was a molten-skinned monster, a Corrupter, whatever *that* was. Perhaps, underneath the skin, this beastly looking man was something unexpected, but in a good way.

The glowing senior fixed her with a beady stare. He looked her critically up and down.

"I suppose you'll have to do," he eventually concluded, then turned dismissively to walk away.

"Hey! Where are you going? Who are you? How did you

find me?" Eleanor shouted, surprising even herself with how she reacted to his crotchety indifference. She was thoroughly sick of being ignored, chased and lied to. This shy girl had officially reached the end of her tether.

"We had a deal, remember?" she demanded a little less confidently.

The man chuckled dustily, amused by her impudence.

"Why, yes we did," he muttered, and turned back. "My name? Well, then, you may call me…Agostino…and you shall see me again very soon."

And with that, he simply faded away into thin air.

CHAPTER 10

Destiny and the Devil

Koemi, Harata and Eleanor were dreaming.

Not at the same time, of course, for they lived in far-flung parts of the globe and slept at different times. Yet somehow, it *was* the same dream they shared.

Koemi stood at the top of a beautiful staircase (and Harata did, *and* Eleanor too). It was carved from polished marble the color of vanilla ice cream rippled with seams of chocolate, and it gleamed in the clean morning light. At the bottom of the stairs was a simple oak door beneath an exquisite stained glass window, which depicted an enticing emerald forest and a group of children dressed in white robes standing at its threshold.

Each girl walked slowly down the lustrous steps and pushed open the door. Beyond the door was blackness, but each girl padded eagerly into the dark, impatient to see what secrets lay ahead. The carpet was royal purple. As the girls walked, however, they somehow became aware of *each other*. They felt the impressions of other presences, other souls walking in time with their steps. If any of the girls were to glance over her shoulder, she would have caught a glimpse of a shimmering halo effect surrounding her, as if a number of different bodies were occupying the same space at slightly varying times. Even more intriguingly, there weren't only three shimmering echoes—there were seven!

Eleanor found herself inside a pitch-black, circular tunnel. After a few paces, she was bathed in golden light from up ahead. Koemi and the other dreamers walked into the welcoming glow and, a moment later, found themselves under an eggshell-pale sky, standing on a bare dirt track. The path was narrow and flanked by a row of graceful evergreen trees that flared up from their slender trunks into perfectly curved teardrops.

Following the path for a short while brought the dreamers to an open courtyard. The air was heady with the fragrance of jasmine. On either side of this space was a worn granite bench. At the center, a figure sat in the lotus position, head lowered, face hidden. A rich, golden illumination rolled off its skin, thus obscuring any detail that might have given a clue to its identity. No words were spoken, yet Harata and all the other dreamers knew they were being instructed to sit on one of the benches. Instinctively, they realized this entity was a spiritual teacher of enormous wisdom.

The figure leaned forward slightly and parted its hands, somehow opening the dirt to reveal a miniature pool of glistening water cradled between its palms. A shimmering globe of gold floated perfectly at its heart, casting out waves of subtle vibration in the air. The dreamers understood that the pool was the Well of Truth and Knowing, while the orb was Source Energy. They knew that the figure had told them these things, even though it used no words and did not speak.

Together Eleanor, Harata, Koemi, the teacher and all the dreamers gazed down at the pool in wonder. Several moments passed, then the teacher passed its hands over the earth. When its fingers moved aside, the dirt had returned to ordinary, packed dry soil. In their minds, the dreamers suddenly knew what the figure wanted them to know: it was time to leave.

A little regretfully, but charged with a sense of tremendous vigor, the dreamers exited and returned along the tree-lined path. They headed towards the all-encompassing shining wall that guarded the path. The light in this place was Love, the girls all knew now. However, when the dreamers reached the light, they found the exit guarded by a robed male figure, its face hooded. The figure bore the scent of orange blossom and beckoned for their hands. His skin was dry and papery, but Harata, Eleanor and Koemi felt pure love seeping into their bodies like a warm, delicious liquid.

Suddenly, the robed man passed them each an aquamarine crystal of many glinting facets. Instinctively, each girl knew that these were excellent stones for communication and spiritual connection, and were named the Stones of Courage. They were used for protection, but also to encourage their users to realize his or her own special gift of service to humanity in its greatest time of need.

The crystals reflected back a thousand points of dancing light, and the figure gestured for the dreamers to pass back through the gateway. The girls obeyed, reluctant to quit the peace of this place, and walked up the winding staircase.

■ ■ ■ ■ ■

Koemi opened her eyes with a little gasp. She was staring at the blank, white page of her bedroom ceiling and felt a strange, tingling energy all over.

"I was wondering when you'd wake up," Agostino growled from his seat by the window. Koemi jerked upright and gathered the sheets protectively around her.

"We haven't got time to sleep in," Agostino admonished, oblivious to her embarrassment. "You children have to learn about your destiny if you're ever going to be fit to save the world. I don't know," he muttered. "Young people today…"

He was floating six inches above the chair in the lotus position. He smelled of orange blossom.

■ ■ ■ ■ ■

"Why do you glow like that?" Harata wanted to know.

"Why are you so pasty and pale?" Agostino asked with a roguish grin.

Harata looked down at her dark-brown skin. They were in her tiny bedroom in Lahore and it was early evening, the sky outside was a dark, plum hue. She frowned. Was this a strange, glowing old man joke? She couldn't have been much darker if she'd painted herself with tar! Harata's brow furrowed deeply as she considered the paradox.

"I think you look like that because you're projecting yourself here and the light where you are is different. It's…sunlight, but from earlier in the day! There's a time difference! I think you're probably in…" She cast her mind back to her crowded and chaotic geography lessons. "Italy! Three hours behind Pakistan, so still in the afternoon sun!"

Harata was delighted by her brilliant feat of deduction and

jutted her chin out. Agostino transfixed her with a shrewd look. Harata found that even a tomboy as rebellious as she couldn't bear the full weight of this old man's gaze. She ducked her eyes and stared nervously at her peeling sandals.

"Well you need to go to the head of the class," Agostino finally remarked, chuckling dustily. "Dear child, you must change those things you are to witness. Do not sway from your duty, for you are the harbinger of peace. Your name reveals your gift—it means *free man,* and this you will do. The most difficult part of your journey is to understand that what is real to others, the tangible, physical world that everyone agrees exists, is not *your* world. To focus on the *intangible* as the basis for *your* reality requires a willingness to be misunderstood by others… You will defy their logic!"

Agostino winked.

■ ■ ■ ■ ■

"So, you're in Italy?" Eleanor asked, her breath coming in short sharp jerks.

"Rural Italy to be precise. Umbria to be very, very precise," Agostino returned.

"You're astrally projecting your mind all the way around the world to New York, but you're *also* talking to other people like me in different countries?"

"Well, when you get to my age you don't get out so much, so you have to find other ways of keeping up with current events," Agostino told her impishly.

"So, how old are you?" Ellie wanted to know.

"As old as dirt!" the glowing phantom exclaimed, which made Ellie exasperated.

"Well, if you didn't really know how old you were, how old would you be?"

"Older than dirt!"

"You're infuriating," Eleanor huffed.

"And you're slow! Come on! Run!"

In spite of her frustration, Eleanor put in another burst of effort to get herself over the crest of the hill. Agostino had talked her into going on regular runs along the steepest gradients in the streets surrounding the hospital. Ellie had been very pleased at first, as she liked to exercise, but Agostino was a merciless personal trainer. What was worse, *he* didn't even run himself. He just floated sedately in front of her, his ghostly, glowing toes hovering inches above the sidewalk.

"So, there are lots of me? Us...I...uh, mean," she gasped. "Children all around the world who can heal?"

"I'll tell you if you stop slacking!"

Eleanor wearily plodded on. "I...I don't understand why it's so important I get fit."

A cloud seemed to pass over Agostino's face.

"I must make you strong, all of you...or else you will not be prepared for the great challenges ahead...and I will have left you exposed to a great darkness. Then I will have failed you. That is why I am hard with you, young one, and I make no apologies."

A chill breeze crept underneath Ellie's shirt, stitching her flesh with goose bumps.

"This is a time of terrible fear, and fear is at the root of all violence and disease in the world," Agostino continued, his gaze like a laser beam cutting straight through to her soul. "You are young now, green and tender as a sapling, but you will grow into a great spiritual leader. Humanity must turn away from fear and live out of love and compassion instead. This is your sacred mission. You volunteered before birth and have arrived on this planet at the perfect time. You must trust in who you are and live in the place of knowing you will heal, but more importantly you will teach, and your example will be a message of hope for ALL humanity."

Eleanor felt weak, her knees trembling beneath the weight of Agostino's words. She—a shy little girl from New York City—had the fate of the world on her back. Agostino's wizened lips twitched for a moment, but it was only much later that Ellie realized he had smiled at her.

■ ■ ■ ■ ■

Cross-legged in a forest grove, Koemi peered up at her new mentor's stern, radiant face. For the first time in her life, laughter was the furthest thing from her mind. Agostino was setting out the future for her.

"There is a movement that must occur, or humanity will suffer the consequences of its actions," Agostino told her with his mind, his lips motionless, the air around the two of them vibrating with slow-moving whiskers of light. "You and your peers were sent here to bring this change about. *You* must be strong and teach humanity to overcome the hatred that pollutes our physical world. *You* must heal people in so many ways. *You* will empower the world's citizens so that they forge a direct link to the godhead of nature, regaining control of their lives and destinies.

"Your sacred purpose is to align the vibrations of troubled individuals with your own through laughter, for your name means *little laugh*. People are not their hurts, their pains and sadnesses. You must teach them that they are one with the light of truth and love. You are a messenger to mankind. You are made only of positive energy. Spread this energy throughout the world and it will grow and expand and heal the human collective consciousness. Send only love to those who oppose your vision, for it is they who will change. Many will go against you, but you must believe in your ultimate destiny and press on."

"But how do you know this?" Koemi whispered in awe as veils of multicolored light caressed her face. "Who are you?"

▨ ▦ ▩ ▦ ▧

Up on a flat, dusty Lahori roof, lying beneath the star-speckled heavens, Harata watched the old man frown. The ancient skin across his brow creased like fragile parchment. Agostino's expression showed true regret rather than his customary crankiness, which Harata was already learning not to take very seriously.

"I'm like you," he began gravely. "Or, I *was*. I was able to heal and see all around the world, and I received visions of great spiritual insight... I thought that meant *I* was to be the one who would heal the world... For all my power, though, I was just one man. I was alone, and you cannot start a revolution by yourself."

He paused and ran a palm across his face as a shadow of anger seemed to touch him for just a second.

"I was bitter for a while and lost my way, went to live by myself in a hut with no roof, eating berries out of the bushes. Finally, after years in the wilderness contemplating my dreams, a revelation came to me. Those dreams repeatedly showed me seven glowing figures—I thought for decades that they were holy tutors from the distant past, but they were signs of the future!"

"I knew then that I was an Ascended Master and that I would prepare the way for your coming. I would provide you with the one thing I never had myself: guidance. You are not alone, there are seven of you, and your voices will be magnified like an echo of hope ringing down the ages. You will succeed where I have failed."

■ ■ ■ ■ ■

On a peeling, purple bench within Saint Rafael's, Ellie jumped with excitement.

"But you didn't fail! You wrote a book on auric healing! It's still in the library. It taught me so much, and the only reason I didn't follow your advice was that Logan Vance tricked me..." She shuddered at the awful memory of her betrayer. "Your book worked!"

"Perhaps...a little...but people would still not believe me no matter what I tried. One man shouting the truth in a crowd is just a madman. He is shunned, especially if he has a merciless foe striving to undermine him at every turn."

"A foe," Eleanor breathed. "The Corrupter," she muttered darkly.

"Yes," Agostino told her in a voice filled with disgust.

■ ■ ■ ■ ■

Koemi flashed back to the horrors she'd seen when she was trapped in the pit with Tsukiko. (At the same time, Harata saw the hate-filled eyes of the slavering bullmastiff and Ellie imagined Logan's mutated features lit up for just a second by that blaze of lightning.)

"But what is…he?" asked Koemi in a trembling tone.

"*It* is the enemy," corrected Agostino sharply. "Your great adversary. It labors tirelessly to sow fear and anger in the hearts of humanity, striving to prevent mankind from ever breaking out of the cycle of violence that meshes the globe in despair."

"B—but where does it come from? How can we stop it?" Koemi stammered. She had imagined the beast might come back to haunt her in the future, but her mentor's words definitely left her shivering with worry.

Agostino shrugged, wearing every year of his vast antiquity plainly on his face.

"Some call this thing the Devil, others the Enemy. I, as you know, refer to it as the Corrupter. No one knows what its origins truly are. It is impossibly ancient, we know that." Agostino continued after a pause, "That which hides in the dark places of the world and has harried humanity throughout the ages. It is more like a spirit, or a terrible idea, than a creature. It has no physical body and cannot be destroyed, which is why it has persisted for so long and why I cannot easily answer how we might stop it."

He fixed her with a bleak look, which Koemi fought to match. Even though he was crabby while she was always joyful, she felt a great affinity for this man and wished only to prove herself worthy of his esteem.

"The Corrupter can take on many forms and faces and can infect the bodies of men and animals to pursue its schemes, as some of your fellow Healers have discovered. It feeds on misery and destruction, but we can still fight it. If we bring about universal peace, then the vile entity will surely starve!"

"But it knows where we are now," Koemi insisted. "It's been in this forest, seen my home—what's to stop it from simply coming back to finish me off?"

Agostino shook his huge head, heavy as a wooden mask.

"No. Your laughter has banished it from this place, and it will think long and hard before it returns. It needs time to formulate fresh strategies. Young one, it doesn't simply want to destroy you. The Corrupter needs to discredit you in the eyes of the world. It lives to obliterate the *hope* you represent, remember that, and that is an obsession we can use against it."

Koemi took a deep breath, desperately trying to be strong.

"I am here to protect you, young one," Agostino said. "It is one of my sacred roles to guard humanity against the Corrupter. A torch was passed to me from another, and so on back to beginning times. Yet still our enemy is cunning and tireless. You need to be careful not to draw too much attention to yourself—it is one of the reasons why Healers were born all over the world. We must face all that is to come bravely and with a clear gaze."

Koemi set her chin fearlessly against Agostino's challenge...as did Harata, without a moment's pause...and Eleanor, shyly, but no less firmly.

The future beckoned.

CHAPTER 11

Captain Kauser

Captain Sadik Kauser of Pakistan's Inter-Services Intelligence agency was worried.

He stood over his desk in the bustling Lahori field unit, squinting at the city map plastered on the far wall of the office, trying to discern some pattern in the color-coded incident pins spread across every district. Kauser was tall, handsome and muscular, with darkly defined eyebrows, and impeccably turned out in a pressed uniform. His eyes were quick and deep and full of cunning intelligence. Kauser had joined the Pakistani military at sixteen. He'd fought in a string of ugly border conflicts and participated in tense UN peacekeeping operations in both Liberia and Burundi.

Early in his career, he'd participated in the Kargil War with India but managed to avoid most of the corruption that swirled around the military's murky interference in Pakistan's troubled politics. After an exemplary service record, Kauser had been handpicked to join the Special Service Group's elite commando division. A superb marksman, he'd gained a chilling reputation as an unparalleled sniper, able to wait for days, hidden, patiently scoping his target until the moment when he could strike with greatest impact.

Now, twenty years on, he'd risen up to command Lahore's battle against sectarian violence and fundamentalist terror cells. Whether he was haunted by the things he'd been ordered to do as a soldier, not even his closest friends could have said, but he exhibited the same icy vigilance in the present that he had while staring down the telescopic sight of a high-velocity rifle on the Afghan border. Kauser's enemies called him "The Spider."

Around Kauser, intelligence personnel manned computers, muttered into phones and listened in on wiretaps as they constantly monitored the chatter of almost a hundred suspects across Lahore and the surrounding rural communities. It was a herculean task, and the room hummed with activity; Kauser stood motionless at the center of it all, the calm eye of the storm.

Even he couldn't see the pattern, though. Over recent months terror attacks had seen a dramatic increase and then abruptly tapered off. *Something* was changing in Lahore, but was this real improvement or the lull before an even worse storm? Were the powers of chaos merely biding their time?

"Tip-off!" hard-working Jattak from the Old City bellowed from his station, his eyes gleaming with jittery panic. For a moment it felt like the whole room shrank down to a pinprick for Kauser, to the view through a rifle's scope.

"Where?" he growled, his gaze never leaving the map.

Jattak hesitated for a second. "Mall Road. High Court compound," he blurted. The tension in the air snapped tight as a drum skin. All the men and women in the room held their breath, peering towards their captain.

Kauser didn't flinch. "I was afraid of that."

■ ■ ■ ■ ■

Within minutes, Kauser and his team were rattling along in an aged police van through the crowded streets of downtown Lahore. The bomb-disposal unit was supposed to rendezvous with them on Mall Road, but they'd been held up by a fatal accident, so it was down to Kauser to assess and contain the threat until backup could arrive. Their equipment might not have been state of the art, but Kauser had personally drilled each one of his operatives until they were some of the finest agents in all of Pakistan.

They would need every inch of their professionalism today, though. They were returning to the scene where Kauser's own brother had been murdered six years ago, in 2004. If Kauser felt the sting of that terrible irony, he did not show it. It was rumored this was the reason Kauser had pushed so hard to be appointed head of the Lahori ISI. Not that he ever spoke of his brother to his team or let slip a single word about his feelings.

"There, take the alley," Kauser murmured, and Jattak—trusting his captain implicitly—hauled on the steering wheel.

The shortcut sliced a good ten minutes off their dash.

■ ■ ■ ■ ■

A man with a faraway look in his eye and explosives strapped to his body stood in the center of the High Court plaza, whispering to himself.

A sizeable crowd of lawyers and clerks in black coats were watching him from nearby. They were hardly far enough away to save themselves should the bomber trigger his device, but they were hypnotized like mice by a cobra. The sun beat down mercilessly, indifferent to their anguish. Beads of sweat shone on a hundred brown brows.

"Captain Kauser, what's he doing?" hissed Jattak. The would-be suicide bomber was simply standing there, swaying gently like kelp in the tide.

"Get these people back to a safe distance, lieutenant, *slowly*," Kauser told him in a low, calm voice.

Jattak and the rest of the team ushered the terrified bystanders away, inching them backwards like a wave of maple syrup. *Still* the bomber just stared glassily into the middle distance, his lips chewing on quiet words.

"One shot would finish him off before he could push the trigger," Jattak pronounced. "You could do it yourself, Captain. *Bang!*"

Kauser shook his head without looking at Jattak. "That's not the way I work now. I look my enemies in the eye now."

He began to stride towards the extremist, much to Jattak's agitation. As Kauser closed in on the bomber—who was a slouching, dough-faced butterball beneath his explosive vest—he heard the man mumbling. The captain assumed he was repeating the phrase "God is great" under his breath, which was a bad sign. It was the catchphrase of suicide bombers the world over, and a precursor to martyrdom. However, as Kauser crossed the final few feet, he heard that the man was actually carrying on an intense conversation with some imaginary second person.

"Yes, I understand," the man whispered in an awestruck tone. "My life has a grand purpose on the planet earth. We are all interconnected on the deepest level…"

The man thought he was engaged in a personal conversation with God. This was clearly a volatile situation, and someone had to step in and take control.

"My name is Captain Sadik Kauser," Kauser addressed the man crisply. "My brother died here six years ago at the hands of misguided fools like you. I *will not* let that happen again. *You* are not innocent, but you have a chance to save yourself and your honor. Bomb-disposal experts will arrive to aid you if you wish to alter your fate. However, there are snipers here right now," Kauser lied with utter cool conviction. "If they see you even twitch, then they will put you down like a dog. Nod if you understand me."

The bomber barely registered a flicker off of Kauser's words. He just continued whispering. Had the terrorists stooped to recruiting the mentally ill for their suicide missions?

"I can feel it," said the man, his voice rising with passion, and Kauser braced himself. "There *is* an invisible life force guiding me. It's flowing through me right now, isn't it? It's in my blood, my soul…"

Kauser had to grab the man's attention, get him to focus on the real world and what was actually at stake right now. He fearlessly offered his hand to the raving extremist.

"Here, you. I am here *now*. You can talk to your god whenever, but look at *me*. I can help…if you just take my hand…"

Kauser's outstretched fingers were rock steady in the air. Over his shoulder, he heard a gasp, the shuffle of boots on pavement, but he knew his men wouldn't break ranks. The bomber began to tremble as if building to an explosion, both emotional and literal! Kauser's muscles bunched beneath his uniform. He readied himself to pounce and try to wrestle the trigger from the terrorist's hand.

Abruptly, the bomber started to weep. He looked up at Kauser and said: "I don't want to be on the side of the Destroyers anymore, I want to be with the Healers."

For the first time in many years, the shrewd Captain Sadik Kauser didn't have a clue how to react.

■ ■ ■ ■ ■

Some time later, after the bomb squad had dismantled the man's explosive vest, Kauser watched uneasily as his officers lead the bomber away in handcuffs. Being denied insight into an incident of such magnitude in his city was intolerable to Kauser. So little of this supposed attack made any sense. Was the man mentally ill? If so, what had his masters hoped to achieve with such an unreliable agent?

The bomber shuffled off in the direction of the prison van. Up until that point he'd been a model prisoner, sitting happily on the ground, grinning serenely to himself. Now he started to thrash in the grip of Kauser's men, desperately peering around at the crowd.

"Where is the girl who showed me the light?" he babbled. "I need to thank her! I have to see her outside my head!"

Baffled once more, Kauser twisted to track the man's gaze. Immediately his eyes fell on a tall, pretty girl of about fifteen. In contrast to all the prosperous lawyers and clerks, this girl was dressed in shabby clothes. Unlike their expressions of alarm, apprehension or disgust, her gaze was oddly peaceful. She was looking straight at Kauser.

The bomber saw the girl and his expression relaxed. He sagged against his guards with a sigh of relief. Kauser immediately knew that the girl *must* have had some deep connection to this incident—but what relationship could a poor teenage girl have with a fundamentalist bomber that she was able to affect him so powerfully with just one look?

Kauser walked quickly towards her. Somehow he knew there was no malice in this girl. Looking at her face filled even this battle-hardened man with a sense of peace unlike anything he'd felt since he was a boy playing with his brother in a stream in northern Punjab. This unexpected rush of emotion caused him to stumble. The girl winked at the secret service man before slipping smoothly into the crowd.

Kauser sprinted into the throng of black-robed bodies, scattering lawyers like a flock of crows, but somehow, impossibly, the girl wasn't there.

It was as though she'd evaporated into thin air.

■ ■ ■ ■ ■

From that moment on, the girl from the plaza haunted Kauser. In the days that followed the foiled bombing, the frequency of terror attacks across Lahore seemed to drop off a cliff. What was even stranger was that Kauser and his team kept tracking new cells. It wasn't as if the *urge* to mount atrocities had dissipated, but nine times out of ten the terror plots simply dissolved like sugar lumps in hot tea. The groups fell apart, or, incredibly, terrorists simply turned up at police stations and surrendered, claiming their hearts were now filled with a "new consciousness of peace". All this was achieved without any intervention by Kauser's team.

Violence plummeted all across the region, though some attacks *did* still flare up. Lone gunmen, or suicide bombers leaping out in crowded areas. Even then, Kauser's team was always on hand, summoned by a tip-off from a strangely insightful informer, and the attackers would normally have conversations with thin air before laying down their arms.

At every one of these almost-crime scenes Kauser glimpsed *her*, the mystery girl, smiling at him from the crowd. Every time Kauser tried to speak to her she disappeared. A less disciplined man than Kauser might have doubted his own sanity at that point, but Kauser never doubted his senses. He knew the girl was real, and he knew that she was the one halting the violence. Kauser became obsessed with locating her.

He even started dreaming of the girl, of surging through crowds of faceless figures as he chased her. Afterwards, he'd wake with a start and sit on the edge of his narrow, neat bed in his neat, narrow apartment, trying to work out why her gaze made him feel so...hopeful.

But Kauser could find no trace of her in real life. The original bomber—who was named Sohaib and who ran a vegetable stall in Tollington Market—had cooperated with the investigation. This allowed Kauser to virtually gut the leadership of a paramilitary group he'd been chasing for years. Regarding the girl, however, Sohaib would only say that she'd come to him *in his mind*. He couldn't—or wouldn't—give Kauser any clues to her identity.

As he talked, though, he made idle sketches on pieces of scrap paper. Sohaib was a surprisingly skilled artist, and these were much more than mere doodles. They showed detailed drawings of buildings, shops, streets...

Kauser recognized the place Sohaib had unwittingly revealed.

■ ■ ■ ■ ■

To follow up on this lead Kauser dressed in civilian clothes, an unobtrusive olive-green tunic and loose, pajama-style trousers. Although he never felt comfortable without his uniform, it was necessary to deflect attention while among the throngs surrounding Liberty Market. Bodies swirled like eddies around Kauser as he rode the never-ending surf of the crowd. All the local shops here matched Sohaib's sketches exactly. She was close, Kauser suddenly knew, and he pivoted smoothly, scanning the street like a machinegun turret, until *there*—

Kauser stiffened with recognition. Perhaps he hadn't needed to worry about creeping up on the girl after all. There she was, crouched like a beggar in a shadowy alcove, sitting like a rag doll, utterly ignored by the passing masses. Her brow had fallen and her glassy eyes stared, unseeing, into her lap. Was she asleep? From this distance Kauser couldn't tell. He took in a tight breath and advanced as he could.

A sense of powerful anticipation swelled up through Kauser's chest. After all these weeks he would finally discover how she—a girl barely more than a child—had been able to pacify his raging city. A speckled gray cat wound inquisitively around his ankles, distracting him momentarily. He put a foot into the road and—

"Captain! Please, stop!" Jattak's voice blared out. Across the road, the girl startled to her senses and her gaze immediately latched on to Kauser. In less than a heartbeat, she was on her feet and away into the mob, then gone.

Kauser sighed deeply, the only outward indication of his frustration he allowed himself. He growled at Jattak for his blunder, but he caught sight of the younger man's face and realized that whatever message he'd come to impart was extremely grave.

"You have to come, Captain Kauser! They're taking over the case."

■ ■ ■ ■ ■

When Kauser and Jattak arrived back at the ISI unit, they discovered it was full of unfamiliar foreign faces—white men and women, Asians, black Africans. They were setting up workstations, pushing aside any dissent from Kauser's officers and shamelessly ransacking his team's databases. It was like a burglary carried out with military precision.

Kauser's own staff mooched around on the sidelines, glowering resentfully at these slick, besuited interlopers. Their expressions gleamed with renewed hope when Kauser stalked into the room, but he froze their celebrations with one cool look. He needed to assess the politics of this invasion before he led any rebellion.

Kauser peered around this hive of industry for the person around which the momentum circulated. He saw a hulking, blonde man in a dark-blue suit tapping at Kauser's very own terminal while he issued instructions with stabbing hand motions. Kauser made a beeline for the blonde man.

"What's going on here? On whose authority are you commandeering this office?" Kauser briskly demanded.

"You're Kauser, right? Captain Sadik Kauser?" The blonde man drawled. He was American, from the South somewhere, Kauser judged. He had blinding-white teeth.

"I'm Channing. Here's the paperwork, Tonto, authorized and signed in triplicate by your top generals. Wiretap authorizations, equipment deployment and overtime can ONLY be authorized by me now. ALL that was once yours is now ours.

We have one target for this assignment, an individual crucial to the terrorist cause—a teenage girl called Harata."

Kauser inspected Channing's authorization documents while his gleaming-sharp mind whirred. Channing's paperwork was legal, as Kauser had known it would be. Based on this documentation, Operation Whisperer had been sanctioned at the very highest levels of the Pakistani government. Kauser expertly masked his surprise. He had no choice but to surrender to this new regime. To some eyes, that might have seemed like an appalling demotion for the captain, but Kauser knew that this course afforded many hidden opportunities. As any covert operative knew, it was sometimes easier to work from within the enemy's camp if you wanted to excavate their deepest secrets or run a campaign of disinformation.

"Do you have *any* information about our target's identity or whereabouts?" Channing demanded.

Kauser met the man's gaze with chilly composure. "Not a clue."

CHAPTER 12

The Big Story

I t was seven p.m. in San Francisco, and the night was sweltering. Liza Brooks was trying to work out how to break in to the charity building on Box Street and if she'd be able to justify it to her editor afterwards—or explain it to the police if she got caught.

She decided just to go for it. A story was a story was a story, and this was potentially the biggest she'd sniffed in years. The truth didn't care about legal niceties; it just wanted you to set it free. No one knew how long they would have the use of their mental faculties, as Liza had learned at her own terrible cost, but after tragedy had struck her life, she vowed always to use her razor-sharp mind to expose the liars and crooks of this world. Liza took a hasty look around the sparsely populated Mission District street, then dodged down a shadowy side alley.

Even in the dark she was able to admire the dazzling murals snaking along the walls. They were painted all across this bohemian district, famous the world over for its Mexican

and Latino culture, its artists and activists. The whole neighborhood was a vibrant cauldron of cultures, creativity and
visionary passion. The arts charity she was investigating fit
in very well with the neighborhood, but that didn't mean it
wasn't also a hotbed of nefarious secrets.

Once through the alley, Liza surveyed the rear of the
building for potential entry points. She cut a dainty, doll-like
figure with long, black hair and exquisite, ice-blue eyes, but
under that porcelain exterior she was tough as nails. She'd
started out her career as a rookie reporter covering the savage
San Francisco gang violence of the late '90s. Her real passion
had always been investigation, however, unearthing the tiny
inconsistencies in public life that masked ravines of corruption, self-interest and greed. Using the respect she'd built up
in those early years, Liza quickly became one of the *Chronicle*'s
most tenacious—if reckless—storyhounds.

The charity building on Box Street housed a hugely suc-
cessful center for disadvantaged kids. It offered local children
a safe place to follow their creative urges. The success of the
Indigo Crystal Foundation was even more incredible when
Liza discovered that the whole enterprise had been bankrolled
by just one person: a *teenage* girl, reclusive art prodigy Eleanor
Canter!

The youth center was a tremendous success, but ever since
its establishment strange rumors had been circulating, mainly
regarding Eleanor Canter's unorthodox teaching sessions. Liza
had done some digging and had discovered that Eleanor and
her mother had changed their surname when they'd moved
to San Francisco six years earlier. It was almost as if Eleanor
were doing everything in her power to stay out of the public

eye, despite the fame her work had brought. To Liza, that was more than suspicious.

Her editor, no-nonsense Evan Getz, had not been impressed.

"You want to infiltrate America's sweetheart's charity art group?" he had growled, gazing beadily over his half-moon specs. "Don't you know that girl's a national treasure? For the love of God, Liza, why?"

"What's wrong, Evi? Don't I always bring you great copy? There's something fishy going on here, I can feel it. There are all sorts of stories floating around about her art groups. She directs them herself, you know? A kid teaching other kids art… Doesn't that strike you as a bit odd? None of the kids will spill the beans, though. They're all devoted to her like she's some sort of cult leader."

Exasperated, Evan puffed air through his lips. He knew from long experience that it wasn't worth arguing with Liza when she had the bit between her teeth.

"Okay, I'll give you enough rope—it's up to you whether you lasso the story or end up hanging yourself!"

Liza peered up at the dark bulk of the youth center. There were lights burning on the second floor, a sure sign that one of Eleanor's *special* classes was in session. Adults were forbidden to join in. Eleanor Canter claimed it was so that children could fully explore their own imaginations without inhibition. Since many of the children came from broken homes or suffered physical ailments, this made a certain sense, and the results spoke for themselves: virtually all the children who attended Eleanor's classes immediately began to excel in *all* their subjects.

Many of the kids went on to win prestigious awards. Children with illnesses showed dramatic health improvements, as did other members of their families. It was claimed this was due to a very special meditation that Eleanor taught to her students. But Liza Brooks had come to believe that if something *seemed* too good to be true in life, then it was.

She stealthily rattled the back door, which was locked, then fiddled with the window clasps but found them equally secure. She scanned her other options until—there! An upstairs window left ajar by some sleepy or forgetful janitor. Within moments, Liza had shimmied up a drainpipe and scuttled inside the darkened room.

She found herself inside a low-ceilinged gallery space where Eleanor Canter's paintings were displayed. Liza paced along the row of pictures—haunting head-and-shoulders portraits rendered in a unique, molten style—and found herself utterly captivated. Galleries worldwide were falling over themselves to exhibit Eleanor's paintings and offering astronomical sums for the privilege. Eleanor wouldn't take any of the money for herself; she insisted that all the art be given away for free or that the profits be channelled into charity. Some of that benevolent capital had been held back, however, to set up this center. It was claimed that Eleanor's pictures commanded such grand fees because of the potent feelings of serenity that anyone viewing the works instantly experienced. That was exactly what Liza was finding now. Staring into the swirls of shades, she felt like she was falling into a slow ocean of light.

Her transcendent moment was interrupted by a voice. Liza jerked back into the world. The words were creeping from another room. Liza tip-toed towards the bright crack of an office door on the far wall. She heard Eleanor Canter say: "It's not that, it's just that I don't like all this secrecy. I want to tell everyone!"

Liza peered inside. Curiouser and curiouser. Eleanor was alone in the office. She was talking brightly...to herself!

"Oh, you're always mocking me! What kind of teacher mocks his students ALL the time?" Eleanor animatedly asked the thin air.

Liza couldn't hear a sound. She'd known this girl was the product of a strange upbringing, but to find her so detached from reality was definitely a shock. Liza wondered what the parents of the kids she taught would think if they could see their teacher now.

"You always say that!" Eleanor exclaimed, and blew a raspberry at her imaginary companion. "Oh, okay, I'll stick to our plans... Talk to you tomorrow!" she said, exactly as if she were hanging up the phone. Eleanor then skipped eagerly out of the room. Liza grinned to herself. This office was the nerve center of the whole Indigo Crystal Foundation. The reporter stepped inside and made a beeline for the nearest filing cabinet.

■ ■ ■ ■ ■

Liza had concealed herself on a narrow, metal ledge that overlooked the teaching space. The office had turned out to be a total bust, and now Eleanor's so-called *special* class was proving just as uninteresting. Below her, twenty students, ages ranging from eight to fifteen, worked diligently at their easels, conjuring wonderful scenes out of their own imaginations. Eleanor moved among them, whispering words of encouragement or advice; it was exactly like any other conventional art class in the world. It was disappointingly mundane.

Every file Liza had checked in the office told the same story: Indigo Crystal was run like clockwork. No corruption, no secrets. Eleanor's session had initially seemed more promising and strange when she'd opened her class by teaching them meditation techniques but then, maddeningly, Eleanor didn't elaborate on her theme, merely instructed her class to break out their art materials and begin working—which was when the tedium set in for Liza.

About an hour into the session, however, Eleanor abruptly clapped her hands and called for the full attention of the group. Her voice dropped so low that Liza was only able to catch the odd fleeting word, and even then she wasn't sure she was catching the full meaning. Eleanor coaxed the children into a circle around one lad, Rakim, who was confined to a wheelchair. Rakim was one of the kids Liza had tried to interview to glean secrets about the group. She hadn't managed to get anything out of him, but she did discover how profound the damage to his spine was. Rakim would never walk again. Every surgeon in the country agreed on that, so what the hell was this ritual all about?

Liza's boredom evaporated the instant the children started to make odd, caressing motions in the air around the boy. Was it her imagination, or could she really see fuzzy dabs of scarlet and gold surrounding Rakim's head? A thrill of excitement prickled along Liza's spine, but what she saw next almost made her drop her phone onto the children's heads!

■ ■ ■ ■ ■

Liza landed heavily on her butt in the yard, but mere bruises couldn't slow her down. She ran away down Box Street like she was being dragged by her forehead behind a race car. As she ran, she shouted into her phone.

"Evan, grab on to your seat—have I got a tale for you!" she said the moment her grumpy editor answered. "This isn't just big, this isn't just huge, this isn't just Pulitzer. This story could change the world. It's the story of the millennium. Better yet, I've got it all on my cell-phone camera!"

Getz only grunted sleepily. "Type it up. I'll read in the morning," he said, then hung up without another word.

Liza knew he was hooked. She thumbed her cell phone's touch pad and watched the impossible again: Rakim Johnson, crippled for life, standing up out of his chair.

■ ■ ■ ■ ■

At six thirty the next morning, having slaved over her story most of the night, Liza received a call from the nursing home. She still wasn't finished with the piece and couldn't e-mail Evan an incomplete article, not on a story as *earth shattering* as this. Even so, this call had to come first. This was family.

Without pausing even to scarf down a piece of dry toast, Liza flew from her apartment, spitting curses like sparks, her little laptop snug in her shoulder bag, the article humming away on her hard drive, embryonic, brimming with the power to change the world.

■ ■ ■ ■ ■

The manager on duty at the Buena Vista Care Home explained that Sarah, Liza's mother, had become unwell during the night. They'd had to sedate her, but she kept calling out for her daughter, so they felt it was their duty to alert Liza. By the morning, Sarah had stabilized enough to be allowed to sit out with the other patients in the communal recreation space though.

As appalling as the account of Sarah's distress was, the fact that her mother had called out her name filled Liza with a terrible, selfish hope, and that was all she could think of as she threaded her way between the clusters of senior citizens chatting together in the sitting room. Liza settled tentatively on the soft chair beside Sarah, who turned to greet this new arrival.

"Oh, hello dear," said Sarah in mild surprise. "Who are you here to see? Is it nice Mr. Telford? Are you his daughter? He's been awfully low since his dog Patches died last week."

Mr. Telford's dog had died in Kansas ten years prior. Mr. Telford himself had died two years ago in this very nursing home. Liza smiled brightly, even though her heart felt like it was filled with broken glass, and answered, "No, Mrs. Brooks. I'm a journalist. I'm writing a piece on the care home and I'm chatting with lots of the residents and staff, asking about peoples' stories...their memories..."

It was a smooth, white lie, and she'd used it so many times to ease herself through the pain of these visits that it barely stung any more. Barely. Even when it was inevitably followed by, "My girl Liza wants to be a reporter when she grows up. I think she's around here somewhere. Plucky girl, always getting under people's feet. Would you mind having a quick word with her? She'd love that, so inspiring..."

Liza thought of the story on her laptop. The story, which could change everything, and how proud her mom would have been if she'd only been able to understand. Tears clouded

Liza's vision for a second and she lowered her face to hide her distress.

Someone sat down opposite them. Liza's face snapped up to ask the intruder for privacy. The words dried on her tongue.

The interloper was Eleanor Canter.

"Hello," the artist said calmly. "We haven't met. You can call me Ellie."

Up close, Liza could see how young Eleanor was—but she also instantly saw that there was steel inside this fifteen-year-old. She wasn't vulnerable, but possessed a quiet determination that underpinned the softness of her compassion.

"Rakim spied you on the gallery last night at the center. I did some digging and asked the super at your building where you might be," she said apologetically.

"You can heal people," Liza told her, astounded. "Completely, without touching them. I was there, I saw it."

A pause, then Eleanor nodded. "I can...but so could you, with enough time. We all can learn these lessons I teach. We all can heal the world...eventually."

"Then you can't keep this to yourself! You *have* to let me tell the world. Now, today."

Eleanor's expression grew very grave, and she glanced away in discomfort. "There's nothing I'd like more than that, Liza, truly I would. But that would be dangerous, not just for me or my mission but for you *and* your family too."

Ellie broke off for a second and gestured towards Liza's mom, her fingers waving gently in the air near Sarah's face. She passed to the woman a sheet of paper bearing one of her trademark portraits in striking yellow hues.

"There are forces in this world...forces of darkness...and *corruption*. We both know that. Even though it hurts me to delay, I must wait until my message can ring out across the whole world and be heard by all people, not choked by the tide of darkness… I can't order you to wait, for you have free will. All your decisions in life must be your own… But I ask you to consider joining me in the great cause of hope."

Eleanor clasped Liza's hand and looked deep into her eyes for just a moment, then she withdrew, her palm grazing Sarah's shoulder for a second as she left. Sarah shivered, blinked, then looked directly at Liza as if seeing her for the first time.

"Oh, Liza! My dear!" she exclaimed. "I've not seen you for so long. What have you been up to? You must tell me everything, a proper mom and daughter chat!"

Her mother's eyes were as bright and sharp as diamonds. The two of them sat there for hours just talking about everything and nothing. The whole time, though, Sarah wasn't able to work out why her daughter kept breaking down into tears of joy.

■ ■ ■ ■ ■

Liza stood outside the offices of the *Chronicle,* trying to calm herself. Evan had been furious. He'd shouted, he'd screamed, and at one point she'd thought he was going to hurl his desk lamp at her. He'd cleared pages for her "world-changing" story, pulled in favors, moved Heaven and Earth to accommodate her. No wonder he was enraged. It really had been the last straw.

So now Liza was without a job, but she had regained a mother. The future seemed like a fast-moving river—she didn't know where it was flowing to, but it sure felt good to swim along in its current. Somehow, just like all the children who attended her classes, Liza trusted Eleanor. Liza knew everything was going to be all right. She stepped to the edge of the sidewalk, ready to cross over to Morty's Deli for a latte and some reflection.

A strong hand suddenly pinched her elbow, and a man's voice breathed in her ear: "Please do not struggle. We're detaining you on behalf of Homeland Security."

An unmarked, black van with blacked-out windows screeched up to the curb and three bulky but swift-moving men in smart suits launched themselves out of the back. Before she even knew what was happening, Liza found herself whisked into the van, her hands tied and a hood tightened over her face. The vehicle rocketed away.

It all happened so swiftly, and with such finely drilled precision, that no one else on that street even noticed Liza Brooks had been kidnapped in broad daylight.

CHAPTER 13

Guide Us Through!

Joyous laughter rebounded from the trees like a happy, tolling bell. Koemi sat cross-legged at the center of a glade deep within the Sea of Trees. It had taken forty minutes to reach this spot, up shale-flecked inclines and down mossy slopes. Without Koemi to lead them back, the men and women who followed her would never have found their way out again. It wasn't that Koemi wished to disorient her followers, but something about this clearing defied any conventional navigation.

This dell had once been a place of utter nightmare. Now it was transformed into a holy place of healing energy. The forest floor was a beautiful maze of pink and lilac stones on a soft carpet of lichen illuminated by delicate shafts of scintillating green light. Seekers of knowledge came to learn from Koemi there. Few ever described it as a pilgrimage—and Koemi gently dissuaded them from doing so—but they had travelled from near and far. No longer was Aokigahara Jukai called Suicide Forest. For a select few it had been renamed Restoration Wood. They came to heal, they came to find themselves again, but most of all they came to laugh.

Today ten people, ten Seekers, had joined her: three sisters from Tokyo who had lost most of their extended family in a boating accident; a middle-aged couple from Sweden cradling a secret sadness that Koemi didn't wish to intrude upon; two young men in suits whose lives had been ruined by a stock market crash; a woman from Arkansas whose daughter was schizophrenic; a German soldier who still suffered nightmares after the horrors he had seen during peacekeeping duties in Northern Africa; and a spinster from Shikoku province whose own body was slowly rebelling against her as the ravages of Parkinson's disease set in.

Tsukiko was there also, to organize and to aid Koemi. She was the one who had gradually built up the secret network that communicated with the Seekers and issued their invitations to Restoration Wood. Koemi taught the Seekers how to laugh. Not just how to laugh with their bodies, but how to channel the joy out through their very souls. It was sometimes an arduous process for people steeped in twenty-first-century reticence; it was difficult for them to let go of their inhibitions, but when they were finally able to find release, the expressions on their faces were the most wonderful gifts Koemi could hope for. Every time there was a pause in their elation, Koemi would offer another stanza of wisdom. Koemi found that she was an instinctive teacher, and words leapt to her lips unsummoned. She suspected that she was merely relaying insights she had gleaned from her higher self during her meditations with Agostino.

"What you focus on gets bigger and bigger," she announced first of all. "Share your happiness and it will multiply... You have the power to create the miracles you see in your mind...

"Their laughter swelled again like a cresting wave, reaching higher and higher, echoing louder before draining back into merry, low pools of rejoicing."No one can steal your joy from you but you ." Koemi laughed as she taught. "Take your power back!"The circle of Seekers sighed as one, and she saw deep understanding glitter in their eyes. It wasn't merely that they were healed. The people who came here were *empowered* by her techniques. Koemi dispatched them back out into the world to pass on that learning. Through her pupils, the healing laughter would spread out exponentially from this small dell in whispering old Aokigahara. In time, it could echo around the whole planet!

Once the lessons had been conveyed, Koemi smiled at the Seekers in turn, and each soul realized it was time leave on that sacred mission. As they picked their way out of the glade, Agostino abruptly stepped out from behind a tree trunk.

"Mother, can you lead the Seekers back towards the path, please?" Koemi asked. "I'll join you shortly."

Tsukiko's eyes darted in Agostino's direction, and she nodded. Although she had not developed perception strong enough to see Koemi's mentor, she knew all about him. There had been no secrets between mother and daughter since the night in the pit.

As Tsukiko slipped away, Koemi and Agostino started to walk in the other direction, chatting easily. They traded fond insults, sparring with wit and ripe phrases as they started to climb the hill to a certain lonely peak above the tree line. It was the place where Agostino had first begun to teach her his wisdom, and where they still sat for hours discussing the secrets of the infinite.

During the steep climb their chatter was more mundane. Koemi returned to her favorite pastime: slyly needling Agostino. She never tired of trying to get him to slip up and give away clues to the locations of the other Healers, her brothers and sisters in spirit scattered across the globe.

"So," Koemi began mildly, faking a yawn. "You're talking to me now, it's mid-afternoon... I guess you'll be chatting with Harata next in...New Delhi!"

Agostino grunted.

"Nice try, young one, but you can't trick me that easily! You are quite warm... And so is Harata. Warm, I mean. Lovely climate for Harata... Well, unless, of course, she's actually living in England."

He chuckled at his own cunning, enjoying his side of the game. He constantly dropped red herrings about the other children. Strangely, Agostino had begun to breathe heavily as they talked, his face becoming drawn, a shimmer of pearly sweat forming across his brow. Odd. How could Agostino be tiring when he was merely floating up the slope? Koemi was the one putting in all the hard work!

"Oh, you're such a big old liar!" Koemi told him playfully.

"It's still too risky for you to know anything about the others," he snapped, becoming genuinely irritable, which was unusual. This was serious, thought Koemi.

"The enemy is stirring and has gone out into the world again," Agostino continued. "He infects new victims every day—"

"I understand that, but you never tell us anything! How are we ever meant to properly FIGHT the Corrupter if you won't tell us the first thing about him?!"

Unnerved by Agostino's odd behavior, Koemi could feel herself getting angry for the first time in months.

"Now... *Huh, huh, huh,*" Agostino gasped, spots of darkness invading his glowing cheeks. "Listen to me, you. Listen here—"

Before he could deliver whatever admonishment he'd been about to offer, her mentor suddenly blinked out of existence, exactly like someone had accidentally kicked the TV plug out of the wall! Koemi stared in horror at the empty spot Agostino had occupied. Nothing like this had ever happened before. Agostino was so powerful, a rock on which all the Healers leaned. He was like Mount Fuji, ancient yet eternal, unshakeable. *Wasn't he?*

Koemi ran a short way, calling out his name yet knowing it was futile—whatever had happened to her mentor, he was in reality six thousand miles away! This only caused the panic to bite deeper.

Throughout the rest of the day Koemi cast her mind wide, calling Agostino's name into the ether, scouring the calm, bright spirit planes for his presence. She knew if he was out there he would hear her, but still she heard nothing.

The next day, Agostino did not come, nor did he appear on the day after that. For the whole of the third day Koemi did not hear his voice, nor did she sense his spirit on the fourth. She quickly became so agitated she was forced to cancel all her sessions in Aokigahara. The silence continued on, leaving Koemi to churn and fret until, a week later on the balcony outside their house, Tsukiko suddenly put down her needlework and said, "You need to rest. You haven't slept properly since Agostino disappeared—"

"No, Mama," Koemi gasped. To think that she could abandon her vigil just like that actually caused her a physical stab of pain.

"Child, Agostino would not wish you to make yourself unwell on his behalf. Besides, you don't have the faintest clue what has befallen him. For all you know he's desperately praying you are well rested to take on a great challenge."

Despite all her protestations, Koemi was dispatched to her room to get ready for bed.

▨ ▨ ▨ ▨ ▨

Tsukiko perched patiently on the edge of the *shiki* futon mattress, waiting while Koemi drained her draught of hops and passion flower. After she was done, Koemi wiped her lips and allowed herself to be tucked in. It was strange and yet very welcome to have their roles reversed. For so many years, Koemi had been forced to play the parent to her mother's grief; now Tsukiko could look after her again when she needed it most. Tsukiko turned off the lamp and moved to the door.

"He'll come back. I know it. I have faith," Tsukiko whispered in the heavy gloom. The screen door sighed shut, leaving Koemi alone with the sharp, green ghosts of her LED clock.

Koemi had assumed that she would struggle to sleep despite her mother's care. However, the moment her face hit the pillow she found herself drawn down into slumber. Instantly, she began to dream.

A veil of weak, blue light poured itself across her bed like a school of bioluminescent fish dancing in ocean waters. A familiar outline stood in that glow, peering down at her.

The outline was inconsistent, smoky, fading in and out like a faint radio signal, but Koemi would have known his presence anywhere.

"Ag—Agostino... Is—is that really you?"

There were no features on the entity's skull, yet the glitters that made up his face assembled themselves into a lopsided smile.

"*It is I.*" The words rustled feebly in her head. "*Yet...I...I am so weak, little one. This is the only way I can communicate with you. It is easier to project into someone's consciousness if they are on the edge of sleep. Their minds are more relaxed and you can easily slip inside their dreams. The downside is the possibility that the dreamer will just dismiss anything you've said when morning comes.*"

"I won't forget...will I?" Koemi asked with trembling thoughts, worried that her mentor might dissolve into starlight at any moment.

"*No, our lessons together and your natural gifts have ensured that will never be the case. That might not be as much of a consolation as you think. Oh, Koemi, my little flower, I...I have cheerless news I must discuss with you... But...but I don't know how to begin...*"

"Why are you so weak?" was all Koemi could ask, fearful because, deep down, she already knew the answer.

"*I am dying, little flower,*" Agostino answered regretfully. The world dropped away for Koemi. She knew Agostino would still be with her after he passed over, as Kamiko, Rika and Kenji were, but the Healers simply weren't ready to look after their own fates. They needed their guide. They were so young and all alone, cut off from each other, strewn willy-nilly across the globe.

"You can't. We need your help against the corrupter! It's *too soon,*" she found herself babbling.

"*It is as it must be, child... But I cannot bear to let you down. That is why I delayed saying anything until now, when it is far too late. I curse myself for that, but I couldn't bear to admit my failure. This body is giving up on you even though my spirit remains determined. So far, you are the only one who knows this awful secret...*" He trailed off, his manifestation seeming even more ghostly.

"Then I'll come," Koemi impulsively told the specter. "I have to be with you. Agostino, I'm coming to Italy."

CHAPTER 14

Slipping Away

Harata was running for her life.

Her battered *khussa* sandals slapped on the hard mud of the Lahori backstreets, jolting spikes of pain through her knees. She couldn't stop or slow down, however. White men in dark suits with hard eyes chased her relentlessly. Even in their heavy clothes they were so fit and strong that they quickly gained on her. The only way she'd been able to keep ahead of them so far was with her inside knowledge of the myriad short cuts around her home. But still they came on, bursting explosively through the curtains of bedsheets drooping from clothes lines across the alleyways.

Harata's scalded breath wheezed, and the midday sunshine beat down like a fist, as if punishing her for enjoying a false sense of security. Agostino had taught her better than this. For the last six years, along with his careful lessons regarding her powers, her ghostly teacher had tried to impress upon her how dangerous the Corrupter was. Harata and her fellow Healers were all that stood between that malevolent spirit and its ultimate goal: humanity's total despair. It would *never* stop trying to neutralize them...as Harata was now discovering.

Until then, things had been going so well. Harata had almost felt like they were winning! At the age of barely fifteen, she had become the hidden protector of her city. She used her powers to patrol the metropolis for budding terror attacks before they had a chance to metastasize. Sometimes she inhabited Spotty or other street animals; often she hovered over cafés or mosques in her spirit form; occasionally she even took secret photos and dived inside those memories to glean vital intelligence. Using her varied weapons as scalpels, she sliced out the cancer of extremism wherever she found it.

Her activities might have been conducted invisibly, but their effects did not go unnoticed. Hope had begun to return to Lahore. People no long feared the sudden roar of violence; they smiled at each other in the streets, filling Harata's heart with joy.

Harata was even succeeding in her teaching. Half an hour earlier she'd sat in a room above a bicycle shop on Mool Chand Street with a group of local women, passing on wisdom. Women often faced domestic violence in Pakistan and were forced simply to obey their fathers, brothers and husbands. Deeply ingrained in the culture was the ridiculous notion that women were foolish creatures who couldn't be trusted with important decisions. Marriage was sometimes little more than a form of commerce between families, with women—and young girls—employed as currency. It was a fact that maddened feisty tomboy Harata. If her powers were to be used for anything, then it should have been to combat these injustices.

So, as well as providing lessons in her own abilities, Harata was helping these women to become active in democratic politics, to have pride in their natural abilities of insight, fortitude and imagination. Many were already long used to subtly persuading the uncompromising men in their lives to consider new ideas. As such, they took to these new challenges with knowing looks and secret smiles.

It turned out that the natural empathy these women had for their families made it easier for them to pick up the healing abilities. Although none of the ladies had yet been able to detach fully from their bodies, many of them were becoming proficient at far-seeing. They had tremendous fun hiding small items around the house, then hunting them down with their minds alone. It was a fun alternative to their somber discussions about women's rights, and the whole apartment echoed all afternoon with the sound of their giddiness.

After the latest meeting, shy, middle-aged Noor Sarfraz, who ran a fabric stall in the market, came up to Harata and took her hand firmly.

"Thank you, friend Harata, for all you have done. For the first time since I was a girl I have thought about contributing to the world in some way. If we women work together, then no one will be able to oppress us again!"

Harata floated home on the cloud of happiness Noor's words had conjured. She was succeeding in every task destiny had thrown at her! Nothing could stop the Healers from saving humanity! She'd hurried down the back of their apartment without a care in the world, and then suddenly noticed a commotion behind her block. Her father, Kedar, and brother, Tahir, were shouting and gesturing. They were surrounded by a group of white men in impeccable dark suits, who looked as out of place as crows at a banquet. Two black vans were parked neatly in the alley, radiating dark malevolence. In spite of the day's merciless heat, Harata felt like her skin had been covered with a layer of ice.

In the years since the discovery of her gift, Kedar and Tahir had become involved in local politics. Kedar was now *nazim*—equivalent to a mayor—of the local union council, and Tahir worked as his deputy. Harata couldn't have been more proud of her family. Both men now preferred reasoned debate to confrontation, so it was extremely worrying to see them so animated.

Before she could find a quiet spot to slip free of her body and eavesdrop, Harata's eyes were drawn to a figure in a Pakistani military uniform standing, stiff with unease, beside the van. It was Captain Sadik Kauser!: the leader of the anti-terror unit who Harata had secretly helped to catch terrorists. She knew that he was aware of her existence. In spite of his fearsome appearance, he was a good man. Somehow, the Corrupter had tricked him into aiding its search…

A shout rang out like a gunshot: "There she is!"

All the faces of the dark-suited men instantly flashed in her direction. Their sunglasses made it look like they had holes in their heads where their eyes should have been. Harata fled, but the men immediately chased after her.

Minutes later, Harata spilled out of a hole in an alley wall and into the chaos of the local marketplace. The street was a blaze of rainbow colors, stalls, scooters zipping by, delicacies sizzling in frying pans. Surely she could find a cranny to hide in there. She hadn't dared to pause and use her powers during the plunge through the backstreets as the Corrupter's minions were literally seconds behind her.

A pair of snow-white hands flailed at her through the hole.

Rigid fingers snagged in her collar, and Harata screamed with alarm, but the man's strength was, ironically, her salvation. The bright-blue material of her tunic tore and she was free again! The man cursed and tried to wriggle after her, but his massive shoulders lodged in the gap.

"Go around! I can't get through! She's in the market," she heard him yell at his compatriots. Heavy footfalls thudded swiftly away. Harata's long hair whipped about as she searched desperately for an exit route.

Her eyes alighted on a cart lodged in an archway. It was loaded with bananas. She dived behind its wooden wheel and prayed for the ruckus of the crowds to conceal her. Her breath came in tight, little spurts as she listened to the clatter of the agents sprinting down the street. She heard their voices bark curtly in English, then the sounds of them making their way methodically around the various shops and stalls.

Harata still didn't dare use her powers, but her mind turned to another potential savior: Agostino. She called out to him now, yelling into the astral plane with all her psychic might. Normally, whenever she called, she would feel the tingle of her mentor's presence within moments, no matter what time of night or day. This time, however, there was nothing. It wasn't just that he was ignoring her. She felt a dull, cold ache that she'd never encountered before. It felt like Agostino simply wasn't there, and that terrified her almost as much as her dark-suited pursuers.

After about ten minutes, she heard the agents' voices move off. Her body flopped in relief, but also despair. She didn't dare return home now, as they would surely have her house watched all day and all night. She was afraid for her family, but with Kedar and Tahir being such public figures now, the

Corrupter wouldn't dare do anything to them directly. She was effectively homeless and rupee-less. What was she to do? She had to keep moving, that was the answer. Work out a proper plan later...

She risked a quick peep out of her peep-hole and suppressed a gasp. Three agents were standing meters away! If any of them turned round she'd be instantly caught.

Suddenly a strong hand tugged Harata into the forest of silken drapes forming the plush interior of a fabric-seller's stall.

"Don't fear, brave Harata, the women of Lahore will protect you," whispered the once-shy, now strong voice of Noor Sarfraz.

■ ■ ■ ■ ■

Agostino and his family lived in a rustic, chalet-style cottage at the foot of the Apennine Mountains, amidst the most incredible countryside Koemi had ever seen. It was a wild, hot, simmering land of stark beauty, chirping crickets, long grass and the golden hues that Agostino had been clothed in whenever he appeared. The light was so sweet and warm and soft against Koemi's brow, the wind stirring her hair like caresses.

Koemi had travelled the long journey alone. The endless parade of flights and airport lounges had passed as a twilight blur, and she struggled now to remember it in any detail. Tsukiko had wanted to accompany her, but Koemi insisted she was fifteen and older inside than many people twice her age. She needed to do this herself. Anyway, Tsukiko had to stay near Aokigahara to look after their network of travellers. Koemi's was not a dangerous trip. Tsukiko eventually agreed. Her little flower was blossoming into an independent woman.

When Koemi arrived in Italy, one of Agostino's great nieces, Celestina, was there to meet her as she got off the plane. Celestina drove her out to the isolated cottage in a battered old Fiat. Agostino had once lived alone, but now his house was—to his great irritation—full of relatives looking after him. He had never married or had children of his own, but he had many sisters and brothers and now nieces, nephews, great nieces and great nephews. When Koemi nervously entered the house she instinctively sensed it was filled to the rafters with life, laughter and joy that was tinged with just a hint of melancholy. Her natural healing laughter rose out of her as she was introduced to Vanna, Calvino, Elena, Immacolata, Pepe, Raniero, Columbia… So many names, so many faces, it made her head spin.

"Yes, yes, I know, I know, I look awful," Agostino grunted the moment Koemi stepped into his sickroom. It was clear how weak he'd become, as frail as a bundle of winter sticks gathered with a reed, huddled beneath piles of covers. Still, he had a twinkle in his eye and a fierce tip to his tongue. "You'd look just as bad if you had to put up with the nurses I've got!"

He was being attended to by his much younger sisters, all in their sixties and seventies.

"We give you exactly the care you deserve, you old goat," said Nunzia, his sister, as she mopped his sweat-dashed brow. She winked at Koemi to show her humor.

Koemi couldn't stop herself from giggling, and all the sisters grinned at her. Even Agostino grumbled out a bark of humor. He managed to offer Koemi his hand, and she shook it gingerly. Finally she had met her mentor in the flesh. It was a moment she would remember for the rest of her days.

Over the next week, Koemi helped Agostino's family nurse the old man. It wasn't an arduous task, and the house was surprisingly full of rambunctious cheer. The meals were hearty, the jokes good and the love infectious, though no one could fully forget their true reason for gathering. Agostino was too drained to handle a full audience of his vast family, so they kept him company in shifts. Koemi was the only one who spent time with him alone, helping him with her laughter therapy and gaining fresh insights from his amazing wisdom. As deathbeds went, Koemi didn't know how it could have been any happier.

But now Koemi sat on a rock, staring up at the ghostly violet mountains towering above. She thought about Mount Fuji and Aokigahara Jukai, all the souls she'd saved from despair, the Seekers she now taught, how far she'd come in her own learning… So much of that was because of her teacher, Agostino. She'd wanted to sit by herself not because of her grief but because she was so horribly afraid. Over the past couple of days, Agostino's condition had declined steeply. It was clear that the end was very near. His skin had taken on an almost translucent glaze, his slow veins gleaming like violet petals. He could no longer sit up or eat, and his eyes were huge, seeming to glow in the low light.

A few minutes earlier, Koemi had stood at his bedside in the shuttered bedroom, holding his ancient hand, which was barely heavier than a scrap of parchment. His voice was as weak as a breeze yet, for once, it was without any trace of gruffness.

"I don't fear death, little blossom. It is merely the passing of one state to another, and we should glory in that transformation! It is not the end, merely the continuation of my journey. I relish all the sights I shall see soon. My only regret is that I am leaving you and all the other children, but I know you are ready. Your true teacher is the quiet voice inside of you. It always has been and always will be with you."

Up until that moment, Koemi had believed that she *was* strong enough to deal with his passing, but his words broke her resolve, and fear came spewing up out of her like a spray.

"No, no! We can't, Agostino! We're not ready! Stay for just a little while longer! Please!"

She begged him through floods of tears, but all he did was smile back at her with endless forgiveness until Koemi couldn't bear it anymore. She fled and ran across the meadow to sit on the smooth stone, trembling with uncertainty. She was sure the Healers couldn't fend for themselves, and she didn't want to be alone with the Corrupter out in the world. She thought of that night in the pit and shuddered.

Now the grass behind her rustled, and she twisted at the shoulder to discover Celestina standing over her with an expression of mingled sadness and joy creasing her face.

"It's time," she said.

CHAPTER 15

The List

A crowd of journalists had gathered on Box Street, across from the Indigo Crystal Foundation charity building. They chatted and laughed, eating take-out food, making endless calls on their cell phones, tapping away at laptops on the hoods of their cars. However, their camera lenses never strayed too far from the building's brightly painted facade. They'd been there for two days.

Ellie and her mother peered down from the cramped, second-story office.

"I think you're going to have to cancel tonight's class, darling," Rachel said, sadly.

Her aura was tinged with concern but, happily, no threads of corrosive angst, as had once so often been the case. In the years since they had moved to San Francisco, Eleanor's mother had blossomed, gradually shedding all her anger and skittishness like layers of winter clothes she no longer needed. She was pure Happy Mom now and helped her daughter in any way she could. When all else looked bleak, thinking about her mother's transformation always cheered Ellie. It proved to her that she was on the right course, and that her teachings *were* helping.

"We can't," Ellie protested. "Those kids are relying on us! And we're relying on them. The kids *are* the hope that will defeat the likes of Logan Vance—a ripple effect of hope is rolling out from those kids across the country. They take the lessons I've taught them and pass them on to their families and friends in secret, who then pass on their new skills to their families and friends. It's exponential. We're just starting to see the groundswell gather!"

It felt to Ellie like they were under siege. When she'd been younger it would have seemed like the most terrifying thing in the world to have the eyes of all the local papers and TV stations in the region on her! She was made of sterner stuff today. She might still have cringed inside at all this unwanted attention, but she'd made a pact with herself never to let her doubts undermine her.

"I'm sorry, Ellie, but if anyone tries to get to this place today they'll be mobbed. We don't want the kids or their families to suffer that. Some of the parents might even stop their children from coming altogether. I think I'm going to have to call around now and cancel the session."

Ellie shrugged and finally conceded. Rachel nodded, then withdrew to the hall to make her calls. What was even more frustrating to Ellie was the fact that she thought she'd headed off this tide by going to see Liza Brooks. She knew that Liza hadn't betrayed her. Ellie hadn't heard from the journalist since seeing her at the nursing home, but when she'd left that place, the pure glow that surrounded Liza as she talked to her mother—who'd been lucid for the first time in months—had convinced Ellie of the reporter's deep honesty and decency.

However, even if Liza hadn't intentionally given away any clues, it was entirely possible she'd inadvertently left a trail of bread crumbs for other less scrupulous story hounds to follow. Not that any of the reporters outside actually knew anything other than rumors, but their continued presence was making it impossible for Ellie to continue with her teaching work and even the simple, day-to-day running of the charity. The human world was doing its best to discredit Eleanor without any help from the Corrupter! The only way to deal with the situation would be to announce her powers to the world, but Agostino had been adamant that it would make all the Healers vulnerable. For some reason, Agostino was absent from the astral plane, and they had not talked in days. Ellie just didn't know what to do without her mentor's counsel!

Through the half-open door she heard the low murmur of her mother on the phone, and she opened up the e-mail on her laptop computer. As usual there was a lot of correspondence from the kids who attended her classes and well-wishers from around the world, but one e-mail leapt straight out at her. She had a message from Liza Brooks!

As Ellie swiftly digested Liza's words, she started to grin. Out of the blue, the reporter was providing answers to all of her dilemmas. Liza had seen the unwanted coverage the foundation was getting and was deeply apologetic. She felt responsible and was offering to take over public relations. She knew all about media intrusion, having perpetrated some of it in the past, and she could easily defuse this storm.

Eleanor closed her laptop with a relieved sigh. It was as though a heavy weight had been lifted from her heart. Liza Brooks was a tenacious ally who would know exactly how to calm this hurricane. Ellie wondered idly if she might be able to persuade Liza to come work for their cause full-time once this was through.

This was why the Corrupter could never win. The evil wraith was a dictator, either controlling its minions directly or issuing orders from on high. Eleanor had friends and loved ones to help her, people who *wanted* to aid her cause not because they were forced to but because they knew it was right. Such purity of purpose could never be defeated. However powerful the Corrupter was, it was just one entity; they were an army.

Ellie skipped into the hall where her mother had just completed her last call. "Mom, we don't need to worry. A friend who knows all about the press has offered to help, and I trust her. I'm sure everything's going to be all right."

■ ■ ■ ■ ■

A stern-faced operative in a low-lit room full of glowing screens and dark-suited agents sat back from her keyboard with a satisfied sigh. She turned and nodded to her supervisor, who was hovering at her shoulder.

"It's done. The meeting is set for tomorrow at noon," she confirmed.

The supervisor hurriedly switched off the high-tech surveillance and paced quickly along an anonymous corridor. He reached an unmarked door and pushed through, entering an unusually transformed space. A wall had been freshly erected to divide the area into two separate rooms with a one-way mirror between them. In the viewing gallery the supervisor had entered, a man stood with his back to the door. He was ramrod straight, very tall but broad and angular, his hair black and perfectly clipped. He didn't turn.

"The details for tomorrow have been confirmed. All teams are full-status ready," the supervisor told his superior. The figure still didn't look around, merely bobbed his head. The supervisor left without another word while the nameless figure's gaze never left the one-way mirror.

Behind the glass, a dishevelled and frightened-looking Liza Brooks sat at a steel table in what was clearly an interrogation room. The figure thumbed a slender microphone and began to speak. His voice was naturally full and rich with a smooth tone, but it boomed into the room beyond as a monstrous, distorted growl, and Liza visibly winced at the violence of its volume.

"Miss Brooks, my name is Venceslao," the figure announced.

■ ■ ■ ■ ■

Not all of Agostino's relatives could fit inside the sickroom, so there was a snake of people reaching out into the hall. As Celestina led Koemi past them, people patted her supportively on the shoulder. The moment she entered the candlelit space, Koemi could hear her teacher's guttering breath, wheezing like faulty bellows. However, his face was not lined with distress, and his eyes were agleam.

"Little Blossom, come closer. I have something for you."

Koemi nervously approached. Using the last shreds of his strength, Agostino pressed a letter into her palm. Koemi began to unfold the sheet of writing paper, but a slight shake of Agostino's brow stayed her hand.

"No. Afterwards... Now...now is the end," he gasped, his life visibly gusting away with every breath. His glittering gaze pierced Koemi's soul, and she trembled at the sacred weight of the moment.

He gathered himself one last time. "I am so proud of you. You are the best of me—all of you are." He raised his voice to encompass the whole room, and they all sighed or cooed sweetly at his words. "You sentimental fools!" he added with a bark, and everyone chuckled at such a characteristic outburst.

He continued in a fond voice: "Koemi, little flower, you are a child no longer. You do not need me anymore. All you need is faith in yourself and the other Healers, your brothers and sisters in destiny. You are ready, even if you do not accept it yet, and so it is time for me to go..."

In spite of the unusually calm atmosphere, a few of the younger step-nieces and nephews couldn't prevent themselves from sobbing at these words. Agostino smiled beatifically.

"Do not cry for me, my loves," murmured Agostino. "*My* journey is just beginning... I feel it coming. The light is here...*now*..."

With that his body relaxed, as if with one single exhalation, the part of him that truly mattered just floated away into the air. His flesh was merely an old set of clothes now, left discarded on the bed. Koemi's eyes sparkled with tears, a glowing veil. She blinked to clear her gaze but then realized there really *was* a soft light suffusing the room.

She exchanged shocked glances with Celestina. It was a pearlescent, directionless illumination growing brighter with every second, though it did not blind them, and they could look at it directly without discomfort. Koemi felt her body filling up like a glass, with a sensation of indescribable peace and warmth. Suddenly a voice said from somewhere both immeasurably distant and close by at once, "*It is done.*"

Afterwards, Koemi and Celestina, Nunzia and all of Agostino's clan stood staring into the light for long minutes as it gradually faded. They were alone with their thoughts yet united in remembrance, some holding hands, some hugging, all as moved as they had ever been in their lives.

It was not until several hours later, when the emotions in the house had started to drain back to normal levels, that Koemi remembered the letter. She carefully unfolded the page and saw that it was a note written some time earlier, when Agostino's hand had still been steady. Koemi's eyes widened as she realized how Agostino had finally trusted her with his most precious secret.

The letter was a list of the names and addresses of all seven Healers around the globe.

■ ■ ■ ■ ■

Liza Brooks was terrified.

She'd been dragged out of the van, still with the black hood on, then walked down a succession of echoing corridors. When the hood *was* finally removed, she found herself in a small room with an en suite bathroom and a bed.

"I'm a US citizen! The government can't just snatch people off the street! I've got rights, y'know!" she shouted at the impassive agent who had manhandled her during the last stage of her journey.

"Not today, ma'am," he replied coolly, then exited.

There wasn't any natural light in the room, so Liza didn't have any way to track the passing time. But some hours later, when she was utterly bone weary, she lay down on the mattress to sleep. The moment her head hit the pillow, however, raucous music blared out of hidden speakers and the lights flashed in epileptic spasms, forcing her to get up. Whenever she was on the verge of nodding off, she was jolted awake by some electronic sound or fury. She quickly realized that they were trying to break her with psychological torture techniques.

She knew now that she wasn't being held by the police, and they were far too well-funded to be terrorists. But what did the government want with her? The only answer was the miracle she'd witnessed in the Indigo Crystal charity building. She resolved to give nothing away, but when they came to fetch her—between six hours and two days later—the continual barrage of mental attacks had turned her into a stumbling wreck.

The new room she was placed in was clearly an interrogation cell, bare apart from a steel table and a mirrored wall. They left her alone for an interminable duration, until she thought they must have forgotten her in favor of some other emergency. Then, without warning, the questioning began.

A merciless voice called Venceslao began bombarding her with demands for information about her investigations, her conversations with Eleanor and the locations of other children it referred to as "the Healers". The voice was a cacophonous drone, treated with some manner of electronic filter. The session dragged on for hours, cycling through the same subjects with grinding, robotic monotony.

"I DON'T KNOW ANYTHING AND EVEN IF I DID, I WOULDN'T TELL YOU!" the feisty reporter screamed back at the mirrored wall.

"Very well then," said the voice with relish. "You leave us no other choice."

The lights began to strobe, then blazed so brightly it was

like a searchlight burning straight into her brain. Liza couldn't block it out even with her eyelids closed. Within the constantly shifting, never-ending wail of rock music, atonal industrial screeches and piercing screams, Liza felt like she was going mad. Her exhaustion transformed the whole experience into something akin to a waking nightmare that she couldn't shake out of. Yet, at the center of this dehumanizing chaos, Liza hung on to one pure act of determination: she would *NOT* betray Eleanor no matter what happened.

But still the storm raged on.

■ ■ ■ ■ ■

As many of Agostino's family members as were able piled into a convoy of cars to accompany Koemi to the airport. She was already feeling small and overwhelmed, but the young Healer wasn't able to refuse these people who had become so close to her in such a short time. Even so, she drew the line at actually allowing family members to wait for the flight with her, and insisted they say their goodbyes outside the terminal. She embraced Celestina, Nunzia and Agostino's other sisters, then Vanna, Calvino, Elena, Immacolata, Pepe, Raniero and Columbia until she couldn't stand it anymore and had to flee into the building in case she cried again. Even so, her heart was lightened to know that she would always have these people in her life and soul. Celestina's last whispered words had been, "Think of us when you think of him, little blossom. Know that we will be there for you always, and come running if you call."

The airport was busy, which helped with Koemi's need for isolation. They say you're never more alone than in the middle of a crowd. She sat beside a large, plate-glass window in the coffee shop, drinking a strawberry milkshake as she watched the strangely graceful silhouettes of airplanes veer across the sky. There seemed to be a high proportion of people wearing black in the terminal that day, which seemed fitting to Koemi. It was almost as if the whole world had sensed the passing of a great light and unconsciously decided to honor Agostino's memory. She smiled at the nearest woman in a black suit. The woman didn't respond. Nothing moved in her face, and that was weird. Koemi's laughter ability meant that she was able to coax a smile from almost anyone she looked at. It was a beautiful gift.

Koemi was left with a lingering unease and decided to test out her ugly suspicions. She stood and left the coffee shop. The black-suited woman followed. As Koemi hurried between the bodies in the terminal, she suddenly had the impression that dark-suited bodies were being drawn out of the crowd behind her like iron filings to a magnet. It was then that her stomach tightened and she understood. The black-suited crew weren't in some unconscious mourning for Agostino. They were the Corrupter's minions!

Koemi dodged through tight spaces and around blind corners, desperately trying to escape her pursuers. She even abandoned her wheeled luggage in the middle of the terminal. There was no shaking the agents, however, and panic gripped her as she realized too late the true danger she was in.

The list! If the Corrupter captured her still holding the list, then it could track down all the Healers within hours. She couldn't just rip it up. She had to ensure it was utterly destroyed. Thinking fast, Koemi darted into the women's bathroom. There was only one stall occupied. She hurried to the sink, feverishly tearing the precious letter from her jacket, intending to use the water to turn it into an unreadable mush. As she turned on the tap she was reminded of her mother's suicide note transformed into sodden rags by her own tears.

Suddenly a strong, white hand closed around her wrist with a vicelike grip.

The woman who had emerged from the cubicle was dressed in black.

CHAPTER 16

Found

L iza Brooks was curled up in a ball under the steel table, her head clamped between her knees. It didn't do much good, but this was the only pose she'd found in the hours of bombardment that afforded her even a sliver of relief.

At one point, about an hour into the proceedings, an agent had come in and calmly injected her with some clear fluid that had made her nauseous and produced hallucinations. Even with all these abuses piled high upon her, Liza had not crumbled. She had not given away one single detail about Eleanor. Despite all the horror, it made her heart sing to know that she had managed to deny the enemy his prize.

The sound and fury stopped, just like that.

"How do you feel, Miss Brooks? Would you like a rest?" Venceslao's voice purred out of the speakers. It wasn't distorted this time. In fact, his natural speaking voice was rather pleasant, though to Liza it was as loathsome as ever.

"Perhaps you'd like some beauty sleep, or an expensive meal prepared by the best chef in the city? A massage? Spa treatments? Well, of course you can—you can have them all, and I will treat you to every one. You simply have to tell me what I want to know."

Liza took a moment to catch her breath. She wearily lifted her head and joked around in defiance at the mirror.

"You're only prolonging your own agony," Venceslao snapped. "You're just a small-time, regional hack. You can't deny me forever. I *will* break—"

Suddenly the voice paused, and Liza instinctively knew that Venceslao was conferring with another presence behind the mirrored screen. When his voice returned, Liza could hear the gloating note of triumph that coated his every word.

"Miss Brooks, it appears that I must leave you now. I have a long journey to make. It so happens that all this fun we've been having has turned out to be merely theater for my own amusement. We've actually acquired your information by other means. Very shortly, all the Healers will be in my custody. Congratulations, though, you *did* defy me…for the good it has done you…and them."

The speaker clicked off. Liza moaned as the last vestiges of hope tore free inside her chest. Even though she had been stronger than she had thought possible, her struggles had proved meaningless.

She put her face back down and wept.

■ ■ ■ ■ ■

The crowd on the plaza roared like a mighty waterfall, their voices all blending into one vast surge. It was as eloquent an expression of democratic politics as one could ever hope for, thought Sadik Kauser from his station in the surveillance van at the perimeter of the square. He'd been relegated to the

B team on what would have once been his own operation. What was more galling, however, was that the dubious new commander—the mysterious Venceslao—hadn't made any mistakes yet, and Kauser hadn't been able to dig up any dirt on his shady links to the Pakistani government. Kauser was used to playing the long game, but even he was beginning to wonder whether he didn't need to shake up his tactics and intervene directly.

He could hear the sea of bodies streaming past, gently bumping the van's skin as the crowd dispersed. The political rally had just concluded and, as on so many occasions before, none of the threatened violence had actually materialized. Venceslao had broadcast his belief that there were bound to be extremist attacks today. Kauser hadn't been privy to any of the A-team briefings, but he suspected this was partially a honey trap to draw out the girl. His suspicions were intensified by the presence of Harata's father and brother on the line-up of speakers. If Harata were present, then she'd managed to remain totally hidden.

It wouldn't be the first time she'd managed to act like a ghost, though. Venceslao's team had been pursuing her for days. One girl, homeless and penniless, had managed to evade a vast, infinitely resourced team of the most highly trained counterintelligence operatives in the world. Time after time, they would follow a tip-off and burst into a cramped back room in the old quarter only to find a bowl of her tea left *still steaming* on the table. They were always one step behind the girl. Some on the team speculated that she was being aided by a secret network of women, others muttered about how often—bizarrely—their teams were set upon by wild dogs or dive-bombed by city birds as they closed in on their prey.

However, it didn't seem like Harata *was* going to escape quite as easily today. Kauser's headphones suddenly crackled with excited chatter from Venceslao's men in the crowd.

"I've got her! Target is—uh, damn, I thought I… Oh, hell, I've got a male subject here with an explosive vest who says he wants to surrender…"

"No. There she is! Get her!"

"Where? I…can't see her…"

"Scratch that. Target lost, but I've also got a suicide bomber wishing to turn himself in. This is getting ridiculous…"

In spite of himself, Sadik couldn't help but smile at the reports of a fifteen-year-old girl making fools of a crack team of intelligence agents. He was especially cheered to hear that pompous fool, Channing, so utterly confounded. Sadik couldn't just stay in the van and let it all unfold without him, though. He needed to change his tactics and become part of the action. He put his palm to the door handle.

"Captain, are you sure?" asked loyal Jattak in alarm, but Kauser was already leaping outside.

"Target is past the perimeter line. Damn! Damn! Regroup on me," Channing cursed in Sadik's earpiece.

Kauser's heart leapt. Perhaps he wouldn't be forced to make a decision that could compromise his loyalties after all. There were people in bright clothes pressing all around Sadik, and the midday sun flared in his eyes, dazing him. He shaded his gaze at the same time *she* emerged from the light. Harata, who had haunted his dreams and seemed to have the ability to prevent terrorism as if by magic. There she was. She was less than three feet away. He could have stepped in and touched her shoulder if he'd wanted to, but he didn't. He just stared at her, dumbfounded.

"Harata," Kauser said simply.

Her eyes widened with surprise and recognition. Once again Kauser's emotions slipped free of their reins and he felt an intense sense of warmth and peace that he could barely process. They were emotions that had been absent from his life for so long.

"I know you," Harata said softly. "You're a good man. Please let me by. I have to keep on helping our city. Please."

"Yes. I don't know how you do this, but I know that you are our protector. Go now. Run, fast!"

That was what Sadik Kauser *wanted* to say, but before his lips had even parted, Channing suddenly appeared behind Harata and grabbed her firmly. Kauser realized he had delayed her just long enough to ensure her capture. His body stiffened with rage, but it was all over. Four burly agents joined Channing and surrounded Harata. They began to march her towards the prisoner-transport van. Kauser halted them with a bark.

"If any of you hurt her, I promise you, I *will* find out and *will* make you pay. Take a look in my service record. You'll see I do not make idle threats."

The foreign agents were not easily intimidated, but they clearly took Kauser's warning very seriously and began securing Harata in the van with the utmost care. Hawkeyed and heavy-hearted, Kauser watched Harata being taken away.

"Captain Kauser, a word please?" said a creamy-smooth voice at his back.

Kauser turned to find a tall, broad-shouldered man with angular good looks and a strangely unmoving gaze staring at him. The man was dark-skinned but not Pakistani, and dressed in a pale-linen suit. He was probably of a similar age as Kauser himself, but it was hard to tell. There was something oddly anonymous about his face. Strangely, Kauser—who was normally so good at categorizing people—wasn't able to place the man's accent. Though he spoke Punjabi extremely well, which was rare for a foreigner, Kauser judged his native language to be English.

"I'm barely a captain anymore, now that I've been stripped of my duties," Kauser growled. It was an uncharacteristic lapse of temper, but his connection to the girl was so powerful that he found himself unexpectedly affected by her proximity and what they had done to her. He was fuming. These people had used him as a live mousetrap!

Venceslao regarded Kauser closely for a second before continuing. "Wouldn't you like to have that power back? The power to do good? To help the girl?"

"Do not toy with me," Kauser snapped angrily. "Who are you and what is your purpose here in Lahore?"

The man smiled with careful humor. "My name is Venceslao, and this is my operation. I cannot explain it all here, but I assure you my mission is of global significance and for the protection of all. This girl, Harata, has *unusual* abilities, as do a number of other teenagers like her all across the world. They cannot be allowed to use their powers without supervision. It is simply too dangerous. For the sake of these young people and the public at large, my group has been forced to intervene."

"But what exactly is your group? Who do you represent?" Kauser demanded, eyeing the man suspiciously. Venceslao's smile crept wider.

"We will be leaving Pakistan tonight, and I want to offer you an opportunity. If you would like to accompany the girl to ensure she isn't mistreated and to learn the answers to all your questions, then you may join us." He offered his palm to

Kauser, who merely regarded it warily. "I want you to join us for the next stage of the operation. You have shown a special affinity for this girl and I think that will extend to all these children. You will be my right-hand man if you accept, and keep them all safe. We will do wonderful things together, Sadik, and learn how to harness the powerful secrets these children hold...for the benefit of the whole world!"

Venceslao's hand was still outstretched between them. It hung there, unwavering. Kauser thought of Harata's face, scared but determined as she was shoved into the van. He thought of all the faces of the men he had seen die during his time as a soldier—some of those at his own hand—and he wondered if it *might* be possible to extend the miracle of Lahore. Could Harata and those like her bring peace to the entire globe? He allowed himself a moment of hope and, in spite of his misgivings, he shook the man's hand.

"Where are we headed? America?" he asked.

"Oh, no," said Venceslao with a sly twinkle in his eye. "We're going to Paradise."

■ ■ ■ ■ ■

When Eleanor went to meet Liza Brooks in the famous Mountain Lake Park, it was a dazzling, bright day cooled with just the hint of a breeze. The park wasn't terribly well-populated at that time of the morning, though there were a few joggers pounding along the path, some picnickers relaxing on the grass and a pair of nearby park keepers emptying the trash cans.

Ellie spotted Liza sitting on a bench and quickened her pace, eager to lay out her plans for the reporter to join their cause. As Ellie neared, however, she realized there was something terribly wrong with Liza. The journalist's normally proud, yellow-green aura was pulsing with agitation. Ellie's heart filled up with dread as she wondered what had befallen the poor woman and slipped onto the seat beside her. Had something happened to Liza's mother? When Liza turned towards her, however, Eleanor instantly knew that it was far worse. Liza was stiff with fear, her eyes staring wide.

"Liza, what's wrong?" Ellie gasped, but Liza didn't reply. She merely handed the young Healer an expensive-looking cell phone. With her heart palpitating like a mouse dancing on a drum, Ellie put the handset to her ear.

"Hello?" she whispered.

"Eleanor Henning, my name is Venceslao," a man answered. In many ways it was a beautiful, warm voice, but Eleanor *felt* rather than heard the cold corruption that seethed beneath those chocolate tones. *He* had found her. Ellie trembled in spite of her promises to herself to always be strong. "Yes, I know your real name, though you will only ever know me as Venceslao." "I know who you *really* are," Ellie said quietly, sounding far braver than she actually felt.

"Be that as it may," Venceslao replied, sounding annoyed, "at this very moment I have an agent with a sniper rifle on a nearby hill. He has you and your friend in his sight. If you disobey me, his orders are not only to kill you but to murder as many innocent joggers, picnickers and nearby families as he can in order to make the assassination appear like the actions of a crazed gunman. Right now, all across the world, my agents are acting in very similar operations. Soon, all you so-called Healers will be in my power. There is no escape."

"I'm so sorry," Liza croaked. She couldn't look Ellie in the eye. "They have someone at the care home with my mother... I...I couldn't let her go, not after just getting her back... I know you were the one who did that for me, but, but—I'm so sorry, please forgive me."

"It's not your fault," Ellie told her, and she meant it. Her mind flashed back to her own darkest moments, to being chased by the monstrous Logan Vance in the unlit hospital. Then, Agostino had been able to guide her back to the light. This situation was even more grave, but Agostino might know a way out of this trap as well. Careful not to betray herself, Ellie opened her mind to the ether and called out to her mentor.

When Harata and Koemi had called upon Agostino, they had sensed a bruised ache on the astral plane. An absence of sorts. It was alarming, but it was more like a sensation that someone had just left the room for a moment. *That* sensation was not what Ellie felt now. Her mind touched a total void where he should have been. She knew instantly what it meant. Agostino would never be coming back. He had left this plane of existence for good and could no longer intervene directly. Ellie drew her mind back and sagged wretchedly against the hard, metal bench. Their enemy had been right. There *was* no escape.

Venceslao had used the Healers' greatest strength against them. He'd used their friends to ensnare them, and it was that as much as anything that caused Ellie to surrender. When the black-suited men came for her, she let them carry her through the park to their van without resisting. It all seemed so very far away now, as if she were seeing events through thick glass.

Inside the dark confines of the vehicle, Venceslao's agents injected into her arm a substance as cold and icy as her heart felt.

■ ■ ■ ■ ■

All around the world, this scene was being repeated as Venc-eslao's noose closed tight around the Healers.

In the highlands of Bolivia, in the Betanzos region, a boy was washing his hands in a stream that provided water for the fields where he and his brothers worked with their father. His people were Quechua Indians, and this region had once been terribly impoverished, afflicted by poor sanitation and contaminated water. Their community had been barely able to grow enough food for a subsistence-level diet. One in two children had been malnourished.

When this boy, Jorge, whose name means *Earth worker,* had learned about his ability to bioenergetically charge water, all that changed. He would fill up the stream with cleansing light, that appeared to radiate from his palms which glowed as he touched the water. This golden light infused the stream with rich minerals, vitamins and nutrients and purged it of all toxins. Nowadays, all the villagers gave thanks for the "magical healing water" that cured and nurtured.

As he bathed his hands, the young Healer suddenly slumped backward from the river, a sedative-laced dart poking out of his arm! Figures in camouflage rose up from shallow dig-ins and fell upon his unconscious form...

In Kyiv, a fifteen-year-old boy named Fedir worked the late shift in the Ukraine Children's Cardiac Center. The center had become renowned the world over for its miraculous recovery rates. He worked as a messenger, so it was easy for him to sneak into the critical care ward, where he raised his hands over the chest of a gray-faced girl. She had been left in a coma by genetic heart defects, something very common in a region where the terrible legacy of Chernobyl still lingered. The teen began to emit the healing energy flowing through him into the girl's ravaged chest.

Agostino had explained to the Healer how living things continually exchange energy with each other, working towards a form of universal alignment. Fedir knew that a person's energy field extended beyond their skin, and ever since he was little, his field had been able to easily interact with others. He could remove blockages in the flow of vital energy with his healing touch. He thought back to a night like this when he sat by his younger brother's bed with his hand on his chest. It was the night before his brother's surgery.

When morning came, this girl would awaken—like Fedirs' brother once did—and she would be filled with the sense of a loving presence, and she would be cured. The boy smiled and turned to go. Once the door was closed, however, there was a loud crashing noise coming from the corridor beyond. In the morning, it would be assumed that the teenager had simply run away to the big city…

In Swaziland, in the central town of Manzini, a young girl lay in bed, too excited to sleep. She had been making hand-crafted necklaces all evening, using the ancient fine-coiling technique handed down by her mother. She employed versatile sisal plant fibers in her industry but wove in other elements of her own design, guided by the ancestral African energy of *ashe*: sticks, stones, roots, bones and minerals, seemingly inert, but actually reservoirs of karmic power.

Able to harness the powers of the Universe in these organic materials since she was a small child, Agostino had taught her how to achieve synergy in her jewelry by bringing together the objects she charged to create single, more powerful units.

The following day, she would take her necklaces to the overflowing AIDS hospice. When worn on the neck, these miraculous bands could penetrate into a victim's life force and respond to information contained in the patient's body. They would balance that person's vibrational rhythm accordingly. Healing energies would continually flow from the jewelry into the patients' auras and then back again, working at ever-deeper and deeper levels to dissolve any obstructions. The girl, Faraja, could barely wait to start handing out these miraculous tools, but before she was able to blow out her lamp, a gust of air extinguished it, and an African darkness fell over her in terror as masked strangers dragged her from her bed...

In Australia, a tall, thoughtful young man sang to the troubled souls he tended to in the substance abuse drop-in center where he had helped out since he was a small boy. They thought he was just singing because he loved music so much—they'd all heard of the concerts he put on, full of strange, mesmerizing tunes—but what they didn't realize was that he was actually reproducing their signature sounds.

Jeremiah could hear this personal vibration emerging invisibly out of each individual's very Being. He had always had high-frequency hearing and been able to detect these hidden sounds emitting from people, objects, even trees and vegetables. He found that he could use vocal toning—an ancient practice employed for thousands of years in Tibetan monasteries, Buddhist temples and in Gregorian chants—to stimulate harmonic resonance and balance the human Meridian and Chakra systems. This enabled those afflicted with substance abuse problems to reconnect with their natural patterns, balancing mind, body and spirit. The people he sang to always left the drop-in center cured of their addictions.

On this particular dark day, however, the young man began to shake and sweat as if suffering from the DTs himself. He suddenly collapsed. Later, the staff and clients of the drop-in center were all too distressed to remember that no one had actually called the paramedics, yet a team still arrived within minutes and bore the unconscious boy swiftly away...

Within days, the violence, hopelessness and despair that had once blighted the homes of these young people returned like a black tide. Deep within Aokigahara Forest, a group of hikers suddenly shivered and looked around in puzzlement as they heard the echo of cruel, distant laughter...

CHAPTER 17

Together at Last

The first thing Eleanor heard was the cawing of parrots, and that was so unusual it made her open her eyes immediately. She found that she was staring up at a maze of roughly hewn wooden beams supporting a low, cabin-style ceiling. Her back was braced against a firm mattress fitted with linen sheets. The light was too dazzling at first, so she blinked her eyes closed. She felt groggy and a little nauseous.

If her growing suspicions proved to be correct, though, this was only to be expected. Eleanor had swiftly surmised that she was no longer in the States, which meant that her captors must have kept her unconscious as they transported her overseas, possibly for days. It made her very frightened to think of how far from home she was, but she forced herself to calm down and take in a few deep breaths to test the air. It was pleasantly warm but not overly humid, and fragrant with a combination of unfamiliar scents—palm trees, coconut, some sort of industrial cleanser—and tinged very faintly with the breath of the ocean.

"Look, she's awake," said a girl nearby. Her voice was bell-like, full of laughter, and she spoke excellent English, though with a pronounced Japanese accent. There was a flurry of movement and Ellie tried opening her eyes again. She sat up. The cabin was very much like a camp dormitory, with a municipal, impersonal feel. The space bore the hallmarks of recent construction: a sawdusty aroma, pencil guide marks, and suspiciously smooth floorboards.

There were three other beds, and three faces peering expectantly at her. Although Agostino had been very careful never to reveal too much about her brother and sister Healers, Ellie still recognized joyful Koemi, determined Harata and round-faced, friendly Faraja. After all, she'd also felt their presences in her dreams for many years now. So, this first meeting didn't need words. They just all looked at each other, and an understanding passed between them as a tingling electric wave. It made the girls laugh, and then words *did* start to bubble out of them like effervescent spring water.

In spite of the desperate nature of their plight, they were filled with such love and giddy curiosity for each other that they just talked and talked. The walls of the rudimentary hut echoed with their resounding delight and amusement. Though uneasy about their surroundings, the teenagers excitedly started to get to know each other. When the topic of Agostino arose, Koemi wistfully related his deathbed words and tried to convey the strange joy of his passing to the others. Afterwards, the girls talked about his teachings and what it meant to be going forward without him as their beacon of light.

Koemi and Harata spoke excellent English, though Harata's accent was very strong and occasionally hard to follow, but

Faraja spoke only her own tribal dialect. However, they discovered, Harata's ability to communicate telepathically enabled her to enter Faraja's mind, where language was no barrier. She could thus translate for their new friend. It was so amazing, thought Ellie in delight, to talk about her powers openly with others who shared similar abilities.

Harata's ability was incredibly useful and *her* aura was the sharpest, most vibrant yellow Ellie had ever seen.

"So where are we?" asked Koemi. "From the feel of the weather, I think it must be tropical."

"That was my guess too," agreed Ellie. "Perhaps one of the South Sea Islands? There are so many and they're so isolated, it would make a good place to hide."

"It doesn't matter where we are, all that's important is that the Corrupter has us," Harata muttered darkly and crossed to the window, which was barred. "The door and windows are locked. This prison might be clean and comfortable, but it's a prison all the same. We were arrogant, we failed, and now evil has us."

Ellie moved to join Harata at the window and peered past the bars. She caught a narrow slice of intense-blue sky but anything further was blocked by swaying palm fronds.

"I'm not sure. I don't think it's as simple as that," said Ellie to Harata. "There's one man in charge: Venceslao. I spoke to him. He was cruel, and he's convinced we're a terrible threat, but I wonder if he's more like a servant of the Corrupter. That would make sense, since there are a number of foreign government agencies working together in secret. The Corrupter can't work directly like that. This is human fear stoked by the Corrupter!"

They all digested this ugly revelation in silence.

"I'm thinking about the others. They must be here too," said Koemi suddenly.

"The others?" Harata asked, but Ellie knew what Koemi meant and answered a little more excitedly than she had intended.

"She means the boys!"

Faraja's face was uncharacteristically grave. In the brief time they'd known the African girl they had discovered that she was gregarious and chatty and forever interested in everyone else's business, but there wasn't a negative bone in her body. So her current gloomy expression was very disquieting. Harata quickly translated her words.

"What do you think will have happened to our parents? Will they have been told...or will they just think we have vanished? I hate so much to think of them waiting, worrying, and my poor brothers, sisters, all the people at the AIDS hospice..."

Faraja's faltering words brought home to the other girls how serious their position was. Harata paced agitatedly like a caged tiger.

"Okay, scratch the question of where we are. More importantly—*why* are we here? We'd be dead already if this Venceslao wanted to kill us. So, what happens next?" she demanded restlessly.

As if on cue, the lock abruptly rattled and the girls looked at each other in alarm. A young soldier in combat fatigues stepped into the dorm. His uniform didn't bear any insignia that might have allowed them to decode which government was holding them.

"Ladies, will you please accompany me?" the soldier asked courteously. His gaze was mild and professional, and he was clearly American. "If you would be good enough to hold on to any questions you have for now, they will all be answered in good time."

Understandably nervous, the girls looked at each other, then obediently followed the soldier outside onto the wooden veranda. The four of them instantly juddered to a halt.

They stood gaping at the colossal outline of the extinct volcano that towered over them!

■ ■ ■ ■ ■

The soldier, whose name was Corporal Deeds, hailed from Oregon. He took the girls on a short tour of the island. It wasn't conducted extensively enough, or with sufficient detail to provide any clues as to how they might escape. Harata inferred that Venceslao had ordered it so they would be awed by the scale of his operation and act more compliantly, in the belief that there was no way to fight a power of this magnitude. He was like one of the gloating and preening master criminals in the fuzzy copies of American films she used to watch when she was little.

They rode in a golf cart, and Deeds threw curt descriptions of various locations over his shoulders like those helpful little information plaques in art galleries: "That's the barracks... Those are the civilian quarters... That's the helipad... The staff mess hall..."

Even though she knew the tour was just mind games, Harata couldn't deny that the base was chillingly impressive,

a sprawling, secret military installation hastily erected amidst
a tropical paradise of glittering waters, rampant, wild vegeta-
tion and vividly blue skies. The squat, gray military buildings
bristled with antennae and satellite dishes, and the avenues
between sheds bustled with tightly controlled activity—soldiers
in charcoal-gray tracksuits jogging in formation, uniformed
men patrolling the perimeter.

Beyond the military heart was a town of civilian accom-
modation huts, an array of brown boxes of various sizes and
utility scattered in mushroom-like clumps. Over everything
loomed the jagged shadow of the volcano, like a mighty god
who had fallen asleep and over many strange eons become a
part of the landscape. Looking at its dark, forested cone made
Harata nervous.

■ ■ ■ ■ ■

Their ultimate destination was an area dubbed *The Gardens*,
which turned out to be a bit of a misnomer. It was little more
than a clearing in the forest where the trees had been crudely
hacked back and fenced off to form an area resembling a
summer camp. There were wooden benches and picnic tables,
a trampoline, a roughly defined tennis court and even a rudimentary swimming pool, as well as huts containing various
amenities.

This *garden* area radiated human arrogance, an attempt
to impose Venceslao's will on the wildness of nature, and it
made Harata decidedly uneasy. At the entrance was a small
detail of guards with a group of civilians whom Harata took
to be technicians or scientists of some sort. Suddenly, another
cart pulled up and three new figures stepped out: a strikingly

mismatched trio of young men whom the girls instinctively recognized in a strange yet intense way that was almost like déjà vu.

"The boys!" Koemi exclaimed. "That must be the boys! At last!"

She instantly started running across the woodchip-strewn clearing towards them. The other girls arrived as she was hugging and kissing the boys. Koemi's power meant that she always made a good first impression, and she drew everyone into a circle for introductions. There was a feeling of completeness now that they were all gathered. Koemi tried to ask Jorge how he was feeling so far from Bolivia, but the stocky, messy-haired lad just grinned at her uncomprehendingly.

"We've got a bit of a language problem," said Jeremiah with an awkward smile. "Jorge doesn't speak any English at all, Fedir knows a tiny bit of English and a few words of Spanish, and I've got some Spanish. It's been a mess!" He laughed.

Jeremiah was tall and a little bony, with the look of a young man who hadn't yet grown into his body and didn't really know what to do with his delicate, long-fingered hands. He was obviously a quiet, sensitive boy, thought Harata, whose ability made her an exceptionally good judge of character. She could instantly catch that Jeremiah had a particular connection with Eleanor, who was also shy, though she had learned to hide it very well and would actually make a very good leader.

"I think Harata can help with that." Eleanor smiled at Jeremiah.

Harata turned away from the circle and walked directly to the man at the center of the scientists, whom she took to be their leader.

"What are we doing here?" Harata demanded.

The man had receding, sandy-red hair and half-moon spectacles. He blinked at her over the tops of his frames in alarm. He stammered and averted his gaze as if he were actively frightened of Harata. He visibly didn't want her any-where near him.

"Uh, we really don't wish to have direct contact with the subjects," he mumbled. "But we just want you to talk, to get to know each other. Relax and play together. There are all manner of games and activities in the, uh, *interaction area.* M-most of all, feel free to discuss your abilities with each other, and use them openly. We know all about them, so there's n-n-no point in being sh-sh-shy."

The man wouldn't elaborate further, and one of the guards escorted Harata politely yet firmly back to the others. It wasn't quite the terrible fate they'd imagined from their great enemy, being ordered to hang out with some new friends. It certainly excited Harata's suspicions—especially the encouragement to use their powers openly. However, somewhat shyly, the teens did as suggested. Even though they were wary of their captors' motives, they couldn't resist the opportunity to get to know each other and even show off a little.

The Healers all chatted amongst themselves. Even through Harata's translation Jorge's honest, eager personality shone through. He was someone who always jumped to help someone else whatever the inconvenience to himself. He was stocky, bulldog powerful, and had the sweetness and energy of a big puppy. He could be just as charmingly clumsy as one, too—a fact his basketball teammates found out at their own cost!

Shortly afterwards, they all witnessed Jorge's unusual water-charging power for the first time. He located a tiny, brackish tributary running along the tennis court's baseline and dabbed his hands in the slow water. After a moment, the sluggish water began to flow with a healthy speed. Jorge actually encouraged the others to drink from it, and despite their trepidation regarding how stagnant it had been only seconds before, it was the most refreshing liquid they had ever tasted. Then, they felt supercharged with energy and returned to their basketball game with renewed vigor.

Fedir was the quietest of all the Healers, and not only because of the language barrier. Jeremiah was naturally a bit awkward and Ellie was shy inside, but Fedir was positively grave, his gray eyes watchful and deep. Harata warmed to him immediately because he knew the world could be a hard place, but he still tried to bring hope to it with all his might. He was tall and strong and slow-moving. His power showed itself in a slightly unnerving way. He walked straight up to one of the scientists—a plump, middle-aged man with high color in his cheeks—and talked to him very intently in Spanish. Even though the scientists were going out of their way not to interact with the Healers, this man seemed to understand Fedir's words and nodded, his expression stunned. Fedir placed his hands on the plump man's breastbone and closed his eyes. A minute later the scientist sagged with a sigh, then stumbled back to his colleagues.

"What happened?" Harata projected into Fedir's mind upon his return.

"I saw that man has a heart condition and told him to see his doctor immediately. I just know when people are ill like that. When I pass by, my electromagnetic field interacts with the flow of people's vital energies. I feel illnesses like an itch."

"But those people are holding us hostage. Should we really be helping them?"

Fedir shrugged. "If we didn't, then we would be just as bad as them."

Harata nodded in agreement, and the two young people sat for a while, not speaking. After a minute or so Harata took Fedir's hand. His palms were much warmer than she would have expected—perhaps as a side effect of his ability—but she liked that.

Jeremiah and Faraja decided to combine their powers in a new and imaginative fashion. She took a selection of smooth stones, reeds and branches, then combined them into rudimentary yet elegant drumsticks. Jeremiah then used them with a set of steel drums they found in the hut. Soon the clearing began to throb with Jeremiah's otherworldly chants, which were magnified by Faraja's synergistic ability to bring healing objects together. It set their stomachs, eyes, hearts and souls aflutter. The music felt like water eddying around them, and it massaged all negativity out of their bodies.

The soldiers wandered around the perimeter disinterestedly, paying little attention to the kids. Their presence was surprisingly low-key and they weren't openly armed, clearly believing that a gaggle of untrained fifteen-year-olds posed no significant tactical threat. By contrast, the scientists watched them with detached interest, making notes or documenting their observations on digital recorders. It felt a bit like being an exhibit in a human zoo, but the Healers were far too focused on each other to let this behavior bother them unduly. In spite of everything, they were actually enjoying themselves!

But then, a chill fell over them. They felt it in unison

and shivered, though none of the base staff seemed affected. Shortly, another vehicle arrived and a broad, angular figure in a dark military uniform leaped out. He headed straight for the scientists.

The man spared the Healers only a cursory glance, but in that moment, Harata knew exactly who he was and everything about his shrivelled heart and the deep-seated fears that had allowed the Corrupter to turn him into its tool. *Venceslao*. Behind him followed a figure that really did surprise Harata: a decidedly uncertain-looking Sadik Kauser.

Venceslao actually turned his back on the Healers as he discussed them with the scientists, who were nodding and making careful hand motions. Venceslao ignored the young people completely. Harata knew what she had to do. She was the bravest, the fearless one, the dirty-faced girl from the streets of Lahore. After kidnapping the Healers, keeping them imprisoned and shuffling them from place to place like old luggage, their enemy wasn't even going to talk to them directly? That couldn't be allowed. Before anyone could stop her—and before good sense got the better of her—Harata crossed the clearing and prodded Venceslao in the back. Like a snake uncoiling, he slowly turned to regard her.

"We know who you work for and the thing that infects you. You can never win. The human spirit will always triumph over despair," Harata told him very simply, in a low but clear voice. Up close his face was all hard edges, as if the skin were flesh-colored fabric stretched over steel panels, but she managed to stare up at him without flinching, of which she was very proud.

Venceslao cold-eyed her for a long time before finally

replying softly, "We'll see about that." Then he turned to bark at the scientists. "Make sure they aren't worn out by this activity. They need to be fresh for tomorrow and the tests."

With that spine-tingling edict delivered, he turned casually on his heel and stalked off. After a moment's hesitation, Sadik Kauser followed him, his expression troubled. In spite of his apparent allegiance with their enemy, the presence and demeanor of Kauser gave Harata hope. He could be a crucial ally if they could somehow persuade him that Venceslao's motives were impure.

Venceslao's car growled away and an instant later, the tingling chill left Harata's skin. She wasn't the only one to be unnerved by Venceslao's visit, however. The scientists also seemed spooked, and soon the teens were unceremoniously herded back to their respective dormitories and sealed in there for the night.

■ ■ ■ ■ ■

After curfew, the girls debated their plight in the warm darkness.

"He's not being controlled directly by the Corrupter," Ellie said of Venceslao. "I've seen that before, and it's very different. But he *is* being guided. It's like a dark version of the relationship we had with Agostino."

Koemi nodded sadly. "His fear of us—of what we might become—has driven him to hate and to let the Corrupter in. Negative emotions are how the evil spirit can possess humans. It is mutating Venceslao's mind now along with his emotions."

"We have to find out what they plan to do to us," said Faraja via Harata, looking worried. "What tests they will do?"

Harata knew what they were all working up the courage to ask, so she saved everyone the time. "I'll use my remote vision to see what I can find out in the camp," she said.

"But won't the Corrupter sense what you're trying to do and alert Venceslao?" asked Ellie in concern.

"I'll just have to be quick then, won't I?" Harata replied.

Moments later, her spirit was speeding out through the wall, past the military cordon, and searching desperately through the most unusual buildings she could find, probing for clues.

Back in the dorm, all Ellie, Koemi and Faraja could do was sit and wait, hearts in their throats. At every moment, they expected Venceslao and his thugs to come smashing in through the door. However, about fifteen minutes later, Harata shuddered back into her body and peered around with wide, frightened eyes.

"They've got a whole lab out there," she gasped in genuine terror. "A building full of cells and...terrible-looking *equipment*... They're going to experiment on us!"

CHAPTER 18

The Experiments

Sadik Kauser was troubled.

Dressed in his full uniform, he strode through the semi-dark of the military zone. Stars glowed brightly overhead while the forest around him hooted and rustled with restless wildlife. He'd agreed to help Venceslao's operation because he wanted to protect Harata, and then the other children. As second in command he'd put in place many systems to ensure their safety, and so far these were apparently being adhered to, but Venceslao's motives were still questionable.

Kauser had agreed to eat with Venceslao and the other senior staff tonight. As he passed out into the civilian zone, he noticed a young officer with a covered tray being admitted into an unmarked hut with shuttered windows. As the commander's right-hand man, Kauser thought he knew the utility of every building on the compound. He frowned and back-tracked to confront one of the nearby guards.

"Who's being held in this building, lieutenant?"

"No prisoners, sir. This building is designated for storage capacity only."

"Then why did I just see a meal being taken in there?"

"I think that was Corporal Simons looking for somewhere quiet to have his food, Sir. He misses meals with his family something awful, so we don't ride him too much about it."

Kauser stared at the man, but he didn't flinch. After a moment, Kauser nodded and returned to his course.

In the mess hall, Venceslao sat at the head of a long table and monopolized much of the conversation during the meal. After the food plates were cleared, he launched into a speech for the benefit of the whole room.

"Many of you are wondering why we've lavished such resources on seven ordinary young people, barely more than children. The reason is that the politicians are scared. It's why so many governments put aside their differences to assemble this unprecedented international task force. Now, they are not scared of these young people in themselves—they all seem pleasant enough. It's their strange urge to teach their abilities to anyone who wants to learn them that is horrifying! In their own way they are fanatics, just as dangerous as the communists who wanted to convert the whole globe to their dogma.

"The politicians are terrified that the world would descend into total chaos if *everyone* were able to use these powers. Imagine what devastation terrorists with far-sight could wreak? Or if the Chinese army gained the power to heal at will? I believe that access to this sort of power *has* to be controlled. We have to understand these people before we can neutralize the threat they represent. Many of you have spent decades investigating unexplained phenomena on behalf of the world's military. Now you have the chance to examine genuinely otherworldly powers at close quarters."

Venceslao's words were precise, his tone sober but resonant, and everything he said was both incredibly convincing and perfectly sensible. The base staff were all nodding along and Kauser, too, felt the pull of Venceslao's logic in spite of his reservations—yet something still didn't sit right with him. He raised a palm politely.

"Excuse me. My country has had a turbulent political past, and today we still have many struggles with the challenges of democracy, but aren't these tactics close to those of a dictatorship? Kidnapping those who don't agree with you, imprisoning them, keeping their views away from the population?"

He felt the room grow tense around him. After a long, blank stare, Venceslao laughed.

"This is why you are invaluable to our mission, Captain Kauser. You keep us honest. Of course, when we know the nature of these powers and how they operate, the young people will be returned to their families. We will report the true dangers of using these powers to the general public, and they can decide for themselves. We'll know more after the testing begins tomorrow, and I would like *you* to personally take charge of the Healers' well-being during that process."

Kauser nodded. The tests were something else he felt deeply conflicted about. At least if he were directly involved, he could influence how they were conducted. He continued to be unnerved by Venceslao. Even if his words were plausible, they played off the worst fears of the others and only served to stoke the flames of paranoia. To deny the wider world access to the Healers' powers and reserve them only for a tiny power-elite seemed...undemocratic..Wrong.

The next morning, Koemi woke with a bowling ball of fear in her stomach.

This was the day they were to be experimented upon. A female soldier escorted them to the shower block, where they washed and changed into fresh, mundane American clothes before returning to the cabin to wait in trepidation. Half an hour later they were led through the military camp, out to a forbidding set of large, metal-sided buildings on the border with the civilian zone.

Inside, they were separated and taken individually to separate rooms where doctors subjected them to thorough medical examinations. The doctors never looked any of the Healers directly in the eye. The building smelled of disinfectant and the cooked dust from the fans of computers. The treatment they received wasn't rough by any means, but what was so horrible about the whole experience was how no one ever talked *to* them. Very occasionally they would be issued a curt instruction such as "stand there" or "roll up your sleeve," but other than that they were treated almost less than human. What made Koemi so afraid about this was that if you didn't consider someone a real person, then you could force yourself to do all manner of appalling things to them. It was a technique you developed if you were a torturer.

Shortly, Koemi found herself in a white space hemmed in by a trio of scanning devices that looked like angled speakers on tripods. At the far side of the room, behind a bank of blinding lights, was a man's silhouette.

"Now. Begin your healing laughter," the figure instructed in an emotionless monotone.

Koemi was quivering, unhappy, unnerved.

"I don't understand."

"Do not ask questions. Proceed with your ability."

"I… I…don't think I can. W-what are you going to do to me?"

The lights burned into her eyes. She started to sweat.

"Begin. Now." A note of displeasure had entered the man's voice.

"Please," Koemi whispered. "I just want to go home!" she pleaded. The lights were so hot and bright that she thought she might faint. Her eyesight was blurring. Any moment now the punishments would begin, she thought in terror. But then—

"This is foolish," said a differently accented voice. It sounded close by. "How can she possibly be expected to laugh in an environment like this?"

A beat later, the blazing illumination snapped off. The newly dimmed space felt like a cool lake on a summer's day.

"Professor Jaydeen, why is no one trying to put these young people at ease?" asked the man Harata recognized as Sadik Kauser. He stood by the darkened lighting equipment, looking coldly furious as he talked to the man with the half-moon glasses from the previous day. The head scientist—Professor Jaydeen—sat at a large computer desk and blinked up at Kauser in alarm.

"Venceslao ordered us not to interact with them!" protested Professor Jaydeen.

"Well, I'm updating those instructions. You heard Venceslao give me authority over these experiments, didn't you? Do you really want to anger me?"

Jaydeen looked very worried by this prospect, but he clamored his defense all the same.

"We were told they are...dangerous," he protested. "We were told they could subvert us with psychological contamination and that we couldn't take the risk we'd pollute our results with interaction. This is a once-in-a-lifetime chance to exploit an invaluable resource! We can't let that go by simply because of sentiment!"

"Are you telling me you plan to hurt these young people just to gain knowledge? I would personally take a very dim view of that, Professor Jaydeen."

"No, no, not at all," Jaydeen backtracked hastily. "But there are security protocols to keep everyone safe."

"If anything unfortunate occurs, I will take full responsibility," said Kauser carefully "You are absolved. Anyway, what harm could it do to loosen your protocols a little? Look at these young people. They're scared out of their minds and barely more than children. You'll get better results if they *are* relaxed."

Jaydeen still looked dubious, but he finally nodded his capitulation.

Mission accomplished, Sadik Kauser went to leave. As he did so, he turned back from the door and his eyes met Koemi's momentarily. A moment of understanding passed between them, then he was gone.

Following Kauser's intervention, things did begin to go much better. Professor Jaydeen came out from behind his desk and worked with Koemi directly. She didn't mind performing her therapy while he tested her with his computers and gadgets shaped like satellite dishes. In a way, it was amusing to watch him furrow his brow time and again as none of his results made sense. Professor Jaydeen—whose first name, she managed to discover, was Daniel—wasn't too bad after all. He was stuffy and officious and still treated her more like a test subject than a person, but Koemi made inroads into breaking down those barriers. By the end of their session, she'd managed to discover that he had a Siberian Husky back home named Wolfie who he missed a great deal.

In the days and weeks that followed, this pretty much became the routine for the Healers. Every day they would be led to the lab block, where they were analyzed and assessed by Jaydeen's army of specialists. In the afternoon, the teenagers took special school classes and afterwards were allowed to play, dance and listen to music. The teenagers quickly began to bond. Ellie and Jeremiah's tentative romance blossomed and they spent a great deal of time talking under the shade of trees, while Koemi and Harata became inseparable, their contrasting personalities—one gentle, one tough—forming a natural fit. Still, the Healers knew that however pleasant this place might have _seemed,_ it was little more than an internment camp.

The experimental sessions were more interesting as they went on, though not for the reasons the scientists had expected. When they'd begun testing the Healers, they'd expected to be met with resistance, but nothing was further from the truth: the Healers *wanted* to pass on what they knew! However, as the girls debated the issue among themselves, they realized it was precisely this urge to teach that was the reason the world's secret services had kidnapped them. The staff always tried to sugarcoat it, but it was obvious to the young people that the world's governments feared the prospect of their extraordinary abilities becoming freely available to the general population. Venceslao's superiors were desperate for Jaydeen's team to crack the Healers' mysteries so that they could control access to them, but this was diametrically opposed to every instinct the Healers possessed. Agostino had shown them that it was their sacred destiny to teach humanity their secrets.

The Healers all made a pact that they would never let Venceslao or his political masters stifle their message. They *would* escape somehow and bring their message to society at large. They had no idea yet how they could possibly get off the island, but in one way, at least, they were beginning to lay down the groundwork: in addition to getting closer to each other, the Healers were unexpectedly making bonds with the scientists. The Healers' natural charisma *was* influencing the researchers, as Jaydeen had anticipated. Kauser's intervention meant they were working closely together in a friendly, collaborative way, and the scientists couldn't stop themselves from slipping under the Healers' positive influence.

A couple of days later, when the girls were alone after lights out, Harata solemnly drew out a sheet of paper and showed it to the rest.

"I found this under my pillow after we came back from class," she told the other girls, then gravely unfolded it for them to read. It read, in a steady, precise hand:

"Venceslao secretly watches you in the lab. If you wish to bring the science team onto your side, you must fool his eyes. Use only your abilities."

"We have an ally," said Harata.

"And we have a goal," added Ellie. "To fool Venceslao's eyes."

■ ■ ■ ■ ▩

Venceslao's eyes, they surmised, were the hidden Closed Circuit TV cameras seeded throughout the labs. Since the thawing of their relations with the science team, the kids had been allowed to move around the facility as they pleased. There were only three or four military personnel inside the building at any one time, so it wasn't too difficult to disguise their activity. Venceslao himself had never visited the labs in person.

Locating the cameras and then fooling them was a daunting task, but they followed the letter's instruction: they used their powers. They hoped that Ellie's aura reading might be able to show some telltale colors, but it seemed that her ability only worked on living things. Then they discovered, however, almost by accident, that Fedir's biomagnetic resonance could lead them directly to their goal. He was actually able to *feel* electromagnetic sources—such as hidden cameras—like invisible jets in the bottom of a Jacuzzi.

They went to work as a team. While Koemi and Jorge kept the scientists distracted with displays of their abilities, Fedir, Jeremiah and Ellie tracked down the cameras. Fedir located them, Jeremiah temporarily disabled them with a burst of sonic feedback, and Ellie stood on guard to give them a heads-up if someone's aura approached the corner. Then the *really* difficult bit began: Harata had to project her mind inside the mechanism and distort the images that the cameras beamed back to Venceslao. This took a lot of practice. Harata had to *think* like a machine, and this was proving almost impossible.

That was until she remembered her very first attempts and how she had tried, briefly, to inhabit an ant. Its tiny mind had been fixed and metallic and inflexible. That ant's mind was the key she needed to unlock this problem, and pretty soon she was able to project herself inside the cameras and alter what they saw at will. She convinced Venceslao that the scientists were still treating them as inhuman *things*.

After the cameras were fixed, the Healers were able to pursue their goal of freedom without any fear of discovery. Their proximity to each other seemed to be causing their powers to grow exponentially stronger. As the days wore on, their healing empathy steadily ate away at the scientists' support for Venceslao. During their breaks, Jaydeen's team began to agitate against their mission. They wanted to confront their leaders and argue for the release of the youngsters. They didn't have the courage actually to defy the military leadership yet, but that would surely come.

Koemi quickly came to believe that gathering the Healers all in one place was Venceslao's crucial error. His plan to remove them from the population was logical, but he hadn't anticipated that bringing them together would actually magnify their powers! If their effect on the scientists continued at the same rate, then spread to the soldiers as well, they soon could be free again to teach the world!

Then, one terrible morning, their plans all came tumbling down. They arrived at the lab to find Venceslao waiting for them. All the scientists were standing around, white-faced and afraid. Panic constricted around Koemi's heart as she stared at Venceslao in the center of the common room, his cheeks dark, lips pale. Hatred poured off him in tsunami waves. Koemi didn't need Ellie's auric viewing to see that.

"From now on there will be a permanent guard detachment stationed in this building. Three military personnel will sit in on every experimental session. Furthermore, the *subjects*—"

Koemi's flesh crawled at the way he said the word. She'd misheard him at first and thought he'd said "objects"—to Venceslao they were the same thing.

He continued, "The subjects will be blindfolded, gagged and restrained when not expressly required to talk or move to facilitate the testing process."

Sadik Kauser was there as well, and he fearlessly stepped in to try to reel in Venceslao's excess.

"Commander, the results Professor Jaydeen is achieving under this current—"

"NO!" Venceslao roared. "No one must speak!"

Kauser didn't appear embarrassed or scared by being reprimanded. He merely stepped back without a word and stood watchfully in the shadows. Koemi, on the other hand, *was* terrified. She clutched Harata's hand in her trembling fingers. Harata squeezed back, but her flesh was cold.

Venceslao was shaking with a fury so strong it looked like he was convulsing. The man looked less and less human every second. As the gags and blindfolds were applied to the Healers, one thought pierced Koemi's fear: Venceslao had lost control. Before, he had been a model of icy composure, utterly certain of his actions. Now they had turned him into a doubting, flailing wreck. It had made him even more dangerous, but now he would be also more likely to make mistakes.

■ ■ ■ ■ ■

Kauser stepped outside and went for a walk to collect his thoughts. He found himself near the strange hut he thought he'd seen food being delivered to. Once again there were soldiers nearby, not close enough to be considered actually

guarding the hut but not far enough away to be doing anything else. He heard the sound of Venceslao storming into his
bungalow. After a few minutes, Kauser crossed to the building
and was about to knock on the door when he heard muttering
from within. Was their leader talking to himself?

"*You said it would be easy,*" Venceslao mumbled through
the wood. "*That they would crack within days.*"

Kauser frowned, trying to make out more clearly what
Venceslao was saying.

"*Falling apart... Not soon enough... Have to increase the
pressure... Lethal...*"

Venceslao seemed to be raving. Kauser had allowed himself
to be drawn into the web of a mentally unhinged individual.
He rapped on the door, and when he received a grunted reply
he pushed inside. Venceslao was hunched over his desk, his
eyes dancing with agitation. He beckoned Kauser closer.

"Now do you see how dangerous they are?" He was
twitching and muttering like a crazy person.

"The children?" Kauser asked.

"Not children—monsters in waiting. You saw how they
were able to undermine people just with their deceitful words!
They infected the scientists with their rebellious thoughts!
They can NEVER be allowed to mix with ordinary people
again!"

Venceslao's concentration drifted away for a second. Kauser
considered his next words very carefully.

"Commander, I need to ask... Are we holding any other
prisoners on the grounds?"

"Only the monsters in the lab," Venceslao replied without
really paying attention. He stared into space for a moment,
then: "Leave me. I have to plan."

Kauser saluted, but he'd decided that he *had* to find out what was inside that hut.

■ ■ ■ ■ ■

The moon was high and silver when Sadik crept through the base towards the mysterious barracks. He knew all the routes the guard patrols took because he was the one who had devised them. He slipped past, stealthy as a specter. He was very concerned that he'd inadvertently put the Healers at greater risk by giving them the letter suggesting they disable Venceslao's cameras. He'd believed they would be able to subvert the science team, then quickly cause a general revolt among all the staff. Then he could have negotiated peacefully to have the Healers freed, which had always been his ultimate goal.

Unfortunately, Venceslao had discovered the scheme. Now the Healers were being forcibly led around gagged and blindfolded; they were banned from socializing with each other or playing outside without armed guards. It was disturbing to see the teens treated in this brutal way.

It was Kauser's hunch that whatever was in this shelter could decide for him whether he would continue to support Venceslao or attempt to topple him. He moved like a ghost through a block of dense shadow behind the locked hut, then began to jimmy the rear window. If he was careful, it was likely no one would check the lock for days.

The latch surrendered within a few seconds, and he slid silently inside. Initially he found himself in a storeroom piled high with military survival gear, but there was a fine contour of light outlining another door and quiet, classical music drifting through the wood. Sadik pushed boldly through the door and found a beautiful, black-haired, white woman sitting at a table, reading as she listened to a small CD player. He put a finger to his lips in answer to the woman's baffled look.

"Don't make a noise," he whispered in English. "I'm not here on behalf of your captors, and I may be able to free you. What is your name?"

"Liza Brooks."

Kauser frowned at her accent. "You're American?"

"I'm a reporter. I've been kidnapped!"

Kauser frowned uneasily. The woman was very obviously a civilian. "What ability do you have?" he asked urgently.

"What do you mean? Stop babbling. I keep asking the soldiers who bring me food what's going on, but no one will ever answer my questions! I demand to see whoever's in charge!"

"You mean you can't bioenergetically charge water or view faraway places with your mind or cure mental illness with music?" Kauser insisted.

Understanding suddenly bloomed across Liza Brooks' face.

"No… But I *did* witness a girl named Eleanor Canter spontaneously healing someone so that he actually stood up out of his wheelchair. I was investigating a story that would have featured her abilities, but I decided not to publish it, so I have no idea how these people found me. Do you know what's going on?"

Kauser regarded her gravely. She clearly didn't possess any healing powers and wasn't a threat to any nation's security. Venceslao had simply kidnapped her because she knew too much and was a hindrance to his goals—exactly as if they were living in a police state. Sadik's jaw tightened, his resolve was hardening.

"My name is Captain Sadik Kauser of the Pakistani Inter-Services Intelligence Agency, and I'm leading the internal investigation into Venceslao's crimes. Please tell me everything that's happened to you."

■ ■ ■ ■ ■

Secrecy was the key to any coup—that and knowing who you could trust.

In this second category, Sadik Kauser had a distinct advantage. He was already sure that the scientists were with him—that was if they could be persuaded out of their fearful bunker mentality. He knew he would need the backing of a significant portion of the military. Most of them admired and respected Kauser anyway, but he required more than that.

Very quietly, he started to tinker with the duty rosters. Over the next two weeks, he gradually cycled as many soldiers as possible through close protection duty with the Healers, letting them meet Koemi, Eleanor, Jeremiah and all the other young people whose essence sparkled like diamonds forever transforming into even more brilliant light. Yes, the encounters were hampered by Venceslao's security measures—the blindfolds and gags and cruel discipline—but, ironically, these actually worked in Kauser's favor. The men and women were instantly struck by how hopeful and magnanimous the Healers continued to be in spite of all the mistreatment they suffered.

These encounters undermined the soldiers' certainty that their mission was just, and they went back to the main population thinking, *How can this be right? This must be wrong.* Inevitably they shared their doubts, very quietly, with their colleagues…and Kauser always ensured he was there to gently nudge those discussions in the right direction.

In every other way, Kauser performed his duties with exemplary obedience. Underneath the surface calm of the base, though, his mutiny was seething. Soldier talked to solider, scientist talked to scientist, they all talked to each other. The ripples spread out, and they constantly whispered, "*This is wrong.*"

It was a month before Kauser finally judged that he had enough bodies to act. He planned to leave all the children and Liza Brooks locked away in their prison quarters. It wasn't ideal, but at least he would know that they were safe in case any sustained gun battles broke out. As it turned out, though, his rebellion went off without a hitch.

He chose daybreak, during the changeover from the night shift to the morning shift. He'd staffed the morning shift entirely with his staunchest supporters and put as many of Venceslao's followers on the night shift. The latter were bound to be weary and dulled, stumbling off to their bunks after a long night.

The mutiny itself was like a display of mass domino toppling, unfolding in precisely coordinated waves. First, Kauser and a squad of his fiercest supporters raided the armory, then his assault squads overran all communications and command points before fanning out across the rest of the base to ambush all remaining pockets of Venceslao's guards.

For all of Kauser's dominos to fall, it took less than twenty minutes, and not a single shot was fired. Kauser sped from group to group, checking that every stage of his plan was completed, then he stood, hands on hips, to survey the quiet camp.

Once his forces were in control and any stubborn

loyalists were either boxed in or under lock and key, Kauser finally went to confront Venceslao. By then, the commander knew of the mutiny, that his authority had been broken, and yet he hadn't emerged from his quarters.

The fact that everything had unfolded *exactly* how Kauser had planned actually made him uneasy. Surely Venceslao couldn't be that easy to defeat. He must have had some hidden escape route or way to mount a return strike. On the doorstep, Kauser straightened his uniform, then drew his pistol before knocking carefully, but deliberately, on the wood panel.

"Venceslao, this is Sadik Kauser. I'm coming in and I am armed, so please do not make any sudden movements. I will shoot you if I need to."

Inside, he found Venceslao just sitting at his desk with his head down. As Kauser moved into the room, he noticed that the weather was clouding over outside—a dark pall had drawn across the window. It was one of the flash storms that raked the island occasionally, often blowing themselves out after just a few minutes.

"Commander Venceslao, as second in command of this operation, I am relieving you of your duties and placing you under house arrest."

"You fool," said Venceslao without looking up. The growing dimness in the room made it difficult to make out his expression properly, but Kauser carried on with his address.

"Your actions are of dubious international legality and are in violation of numerous human rights conventions."

As Kauser was speaking, the first cracks of thunder began booming outside with an earth-shattering report. Kauser thought he heard shouts, but he tuned those out to push on to the end of his speech.

"Once the base has been secured, I will be contacting all

sponsoring governments to open negotiations with regard to the status of the Healers. I will be insisting they be returned to their native lands or other locations of their choosing."

Venceslao didn't say anything. He simply started to laugh to himself in a gloating snicker. The storm had now thrown the room into almost total blackness. The rumbling of the thunder seemed to be rolling on and on and on, and the shouts outside sounded more like...screams.

It struck Kauser like a blow between the eyes. *This* was no ordinary storm.

"What's happening?" Kauser bellowed at Venceslao. "Are you responsible for this?"

The defeated commander merely smiled in the dim light, his eyes flat and unresponsive. Kauser roared and bolted through the front door.

Outside, even Kauser's iron emotional discipline faltered as he stared up, up into the sky. Above him, in a mighty geyser of lava and ash, the supposedly extinct volcano was erupting.

CHAPTER 19

A Blaze of Fury

The walls of the girls' prison shook like cardboard in a wind tunnel. The floorboards beneath their feet trembled as if a full-scale earthquake had hit, and Koemi feared she would lose her footing. Sawdust and dirt rained down from the ceiling in dusty waterfalls with every tremor.

Suddenly, the glass in the windows ruptured, showering them with fragments. The girls all screamed. Black smoke began to flood in. It filled up the dorm with horrifying speed, causing their eyes to tear and making the girls cough. They flattened themselves low to the ground, where the smog was thinnest. In the gloom, they managed to find each other and cling together in fear.

Even though the glass of the windows had shattered the bars still held, and the door remained firmly locked. They were trapped! If they couldn't find a way out, they would quickly choke. Koemi shook like a leaf against Faraja's side. They were going to die!

"Stay calm!" Harata was shouting. Faraja wailed in her own language, but Harata didn't have time to translate.

"It'll be okay. If we just focus, we can find a way out of this," Ellie was whispering urgently into Koemi's hair, but the Japanese girl heard the strain in her friend's voice. The smoke was pressing close like branches in the densest part of a forest...

That was when Koemi suddenly became calm. Instantly, she imagined the smog was the dark of Aokigahara Forest, and relief poured through her. The Sea of Trees might have been forbidding to others, but to her it felt like home. This enabled her to say, "Listen to my voice, everybody. Think of your most happy memory."

The other girls frowned, but one by one they realized what Koemi was trying to do and closed their eyes. They all smiled as they each latched on to appropriate recollections.

"Our thoughts are the strongest force in the Universe," said Koemi with a giggle. "We can defeat anything..."

Quickly, Koemi managed to banish all her friends' fears, allowing them to focus on escape routes. Eleanor's fixed stare became glazed, and a moment later she had tweaked all their auric fields so that they could see and breathe more clearly in the gagging fumes. Faraja located some of her healing stones and swiftly charged them up to protect the Healers. Koemi felt the appalling heat against her skin ease a little.

"I'll project my mind beyond the walls and work out what's happening," said Harata bravely, and her body went slack against their arms. Even using their powers, Koemi had started to feel a little lightheaded because of the smoke. Moments later, Harata stiffened as her consciousness returned. She appeared very shaken.

"The volcano is erupting," she gasped. Koemi and the others swapped amazed looks.

"But there is a way to escape," the Pakistani girl continued.

"There's a lava flow heading this way. If we're quick and use our abilities we can get out when it burns through the wall!"

This was a terrifically dangerous scheme, but the girls knew there was no other way out, and they were convinced they could do this. With grim determination, they set about coordinating their abilities while the lava flow crept nearer and nearer. Harata's spirit form hung outside, providing them with moment-by-moment updates. She began a countdown.

"Ten…nine…eight…"

The planking of the walls flamed and charred as they roasted from the outside and began to crack apart. Within minutes a whole corner of the building had started to sag, then gradually cave-in—and a river of lava was actually starting to roll through the building!

"All right, get ready," warned Eleanor. Her auric sight was minutely attuned to the decomposition of the wood.

"*Now!*"

With each of the girls wearing one of Faraja's protective necklaces, and with their auras strengthened by Ellie, so it felt like a cool breeze was constantly brushing over their cheeks, the Healers charged at the most weakened section of wall—and broke straight through it! They emerged in a cloud of scorched, brittle timbers just as the whole structure crashed down behind them.

Outside, it was like taking a step straight into a nightmare. There was no logic or reason to what they were seeing. It was early in the morning, yet the sky was dark as midnight and the very air burned their lungs the instant they breathed it. Koemi cowered. Deadly rivers of molten rock advanced through the wrecks of buildings as the base was engulfed by showers of flaming embers raining down from the whirlpools of smog overhead. They heard shouts in the dark all around them—the terrible screams of the wounded or dying. This was Hell itself, and they were in the heart of it with no visible path back to the light.

The whole area around the base was cloaked in shifting curtains of dense ash that made it impossible to see farther than a few feet in front of them. The heat from the lava was like standing in a furnace, a constant physical pressure shoving at their bodies in unbearable waves. The girls decided that it would be far more dangerous to stay out in the open. They needed to press on.

As they tentatively picked a trail through the smoldering debris and cherry-red lava flows, they were suddenly startled by blood-curdling roars in the smog, sounding as if they came from the throats of dragons or dinosaurs or mythological beasts. Koemi glimpsed a ten-foot-tall outline with fiery eyes stalking amidst the blackness. The creature turned its head to glare at her, and for an instant, Koemi was assaulted by a deluge of appalling images. She moaned, but the thing moved off and the images quickly faded.

The Healers clutched tighter to each other and pushed ahead. A short while later, a man in a torn military uniform stumbled out onto the path in front of them. His wild eyes swept across them, but he was lost in his own terror and seemingly could not see them.

"No! I didn't mean to do it! I was just following orders! You can't make me go back into the darkness!" he screamed, then dived back into the smoke. The girls carried on, but suddenly three demonic figures burst out of the ash clouds right next to them! The girls screamed, but the beasts *passed straight through them,* their ragged limbs parting and reforming like filthy mist. The specters disappeared into the ash to pursue the soldier.

A short while later, the girls heard him shrieking in horror, but in the next moment those cries veered off into horrendous agony. After a while, the dreadful screeches fell mercifully silent, but with an awful suddenness. The Healers saw the ruby throb of a lava river through the veils of smoke and detected a ghastly, burnt stench. They all *knew.* Koemi wept a little, and Ellie held her tightly to comfort her, but there was nothing else they could do for the man. They had to carry on.

It was clear that this was the Corrupter's doing. Like the Corrupter itself, the phantoms weren't physical. They couldn't claw or eat the Healers, but they preyed on human fear. They excited horror in their victims, then fed on the despair it produced in a horrible loop.

Suddenly, monstrous silhouettes loomed through the smog ahead of the girls. Even though she knew they were just the Corrupter's projections, Koemi couldn't stop herself from gasping in fear, then—

"Koemi! Harata! Ellie! Faraja!" a voice called out. It was Jeremiah!

To the girls' delight, they now saw the boys plunging through the seething darkness towards them, resolving from demonic shapes into their own human forms. In seconds they were all hugging as if they'd not seen one another for years rather than hours. They debated their next steps.

"We have to make it out of this ash," Harata insisted. "We could be killed by falling rock or magma at any moment. It's too dangerous to stay here!"

"If we'd ever been to a dock or a beach we might be able to steal a boat or send a signal. At least it would be a relief from this terrible place," Jeremiah muttered.

"All this is the Corrupter's doing," said Fedir through Harata. "It sensed that we were about to bring hope back to these people. This is its last desperate act!"

The others nodded in agreement, but Faraja looked very uncertain in the gloom. Harata translated her words: "What about the monsters?"

"I…I don't think those things are real," Ellie told her haltingly. "They're just phantoms…illusions the Corrupter is using to frighten people!"

Koemi stared into the fiery gloom, her eyes wide as saucers.

"But they're driving people to their deaths!" she exclaimed. "Right now the Corrupter is killing people before our very eyes, causing them to be terrified, then feeding off that fear! That's how it gains power, through human terror! We have to help them!"

In spite of their own very natural apprehension, it was left to these teenagers to save as many of their former captors as possible. They all agreed that they had to round up as many adults as they could find, rather than just save themselves. It was what Agostino would have wanted. So, they made a fresh start back into the heart of the smog, searching through the smoldering wrecks of buildings, among the trees and rocks and anywhere else frightened people might have tried to find shelter. Jorge drew healing waters up from deep beneath the soil's crust to cool the air—it eddied in clouds of steam around them—while Fedir used concentrated bursts of electromagnetic vibration to keep the lava flows at bay. Eleanor's auric sight showed them the way, picking out the stuttering colors of survivors through the impenetrable smoke.

They found soldiers in twos and threes or alone, dressed in burnt uniforms, eyes bulging with terror. They also found members of the science team, some of whom were near catatonic. Very gently, the Healers coaxed these broken souls to follow them. Soon they had rounded up a crowd of about twenty-five. They decided to lead these survivors into the trees for at least some measure of protection. They set off again with Healers stationed at front, back and sides to warn of danger or fend off any attacks by the Corrupter's ghouls.

Miraculously, after a short while, they encountered a frail column of people trudging in the *other* direction. This group was being led by Sadik Kauser and Liza Brooks. Ellie cried out and ran to embrace Liza, who hugged her back, tears making tracks down her soot-stained face. Tough Harata squared up to her decisively efficient countryman.

"You sent us the letter," she said.

Kauser nodded.

"I think it only made things worse, but that is in the past now. We all have to work together to survive, regardless of our differences. We just need to trust each other."

Harata nodded in agreement, though she did already trust this grim yet noble man."We should gather in a central location that people will be drawn to," Kauser insisted. "The mess hall is still intact, and it's the most robust building on the base. Let's go there."

It was a good idea, and soon the Healers were escorting the limping, wretched survivors towards the sturdy building.

■ ■ ■ ■ ■

With the help of Sadik and Liza, the Healers eventually managed to herd their steadily swelling crowd of shell-shocked
survivors into the mess hall. Soon the long tables were filled
with trembling bodies under blankets salvaged from the bed-
ding closet. The Healers and Kauser used the durable building
as their staging ground for repeated forays back out into the
darkness to gather any more stragglers they could find. It was
scary, filthy, nerve-shredding work, but they did find lost and
frightened people with every new sortie. As the black morning
wore on, they collected Professor Jaydeen, soot-stained,
blinking and bleary-eyed without his glasses, along with a
number of the men and women who'd been their personal
guards and had formed the core of Kauser's rebellion.

After their last trip, Ellie, Koemi, Faraja, Jeremiah, Jorge,
Harata and Fedir sat together on a bench, trying to recover
their energy. Sadik Kauser joined them. He nodded back at the
most recent survivors.

"I think that's the last of them... We're still down on our
head count, but no one else could have survived out there. I
propose we move everyone down to the dock. Venceslao keeps
a yacht that can easily hold this many. It'll be tough, but I think
we can make it in half an hour with luck—"

Harata shouted out in panic and suddenly jerked awake.

"Captain Kauser, the outside wall has broken through! It
was totally without warning... I think the Corrupter must
have fooled my vision somehow. We're surrounded! There's a
lake of lava between us and the forest!"

CHAPTER 20

One Purpose

Jorge, Faraja and Jeremiah were trying desperately to keep the fiery perimeter back with a combination of their powers. However, in spite of their throwing all their energies into the task, the bright, deadly tide lapped ever closer. The other survivors stared in hope and disbelief at the Healers, moaning in fear, feverishly willing them to succeed, but the violent might of nature was too great even for the abilities of these remarkable kids. They couldn't fight back an angry volcano forever.

"It's not working," Harata warned. "It's slower than it was, but the lava will still overrun us in minutes."

Sadik Kauser strode among the frightened adults, dispensing survival tips for the forest, should they ever reach it. Watching Kauser and Liza and all the survivors—terrified yet calmly remaining brave—and all the other Healers—so young and yet so dedicated—a grim pride swelled inside Ellie's chest. If they were to die there, then at least they would have shown how bright the human spirit could blaze in the midst of adversity. They would never give up trying. They would work together to the end.

Together.

The word rung inside her mind like the note of a struck bell. With it the answer to their predicament unfolded in her mind. She thought of her friends back in the hospital in New York and how they'd worked together to heal Cody. She remembered Koemi's tales of her darkest moments in the pit and how only with her mother's strength could they finally drive back *The Whisperer* in the darkness.

Working together magnified their power exponentially...

"We can't do it on our own!" she suddenly exclaimed, startling the others. Baffled looks flashed in her direction.

"Merely using our *own* abilities isn't going to be enough to save us. We must live up to the central promise of those gifts. We have to *teach* everyone in this room how to use these same powers that are inherent in *every* human being. If we ALL work together we'll have enough energy to push back the lava, I'm sure of it!"

The Healers all looked to Ellie with gleaming eyes. They knew. They understood that they had to fulfil their destiny and become the leaders Agostino knew they could be...and they had to do it in less than half an hour!

When they told Sadik what they had planned, he believed them immediately. He believed *in* them and started to organize the other survivors into teams to learn their various techniques. While each Healer hurriedly drew in a huddle of apprentices, Liza Brooks feverishly flitted from group to group, documenting the desperate drama with her cell-phone camera. It was an incredible sight to see: the survivors describing colored arcs in the air, laughing with pure spiritual joy that left pearly, glowing afterimages, causing glittering water to stream out of the ground beneath their feet, moving pebbles and other small objects with potent magnetic forces. It was astounding how quickly these new skills leapt out of the survivors, just like they'd been waiting for the keys to unlock them.

Still, the teaching was moving too slowly. Tension added an amazing urgency to the survivors' assimilation of these powers, but the lava had already begun to sear the walls, and the people were only just beginning to understand their roles. Harata could smell the building blocks, and acrid fumes were pouring in like gray waterfalls through the windows.

"Come on!" she shouted, her eyes unfocused as she peered beyond the walls. "It must be now! We MUST begin!"

It started as a barely perceptible hum, a wavering bass thread, then, gradually, the voices of the pupils grew stronger. Jeremiah's tonal waves spread out as powerful vocal pulses. Next came the magnetic resonance that made the walls tremble and quake. After that, the rich, cleansing steam formed, and on and on...

It was working! The healing powers were flourishing in *all* the survivors! Ellie ran to the window and used her auric sight. It was like a movie special effect made real. The sea of lava was...parting.

"Yes! Yes! That's it, all together! It's working!" she screamed in hope and joy.

With agonizing, toffee-like slowness, the lake of lava unzipped, peeling back until there was a clear passage through the center of the flame. It was lined with parched mud that cracked and sizzled disturbingly, but it *was* there. Working together, their hearts and breaths and minds as one, they had cleared a road to freedom.

"COME ON!" bellowed Sadik Kauser. "We must leave before the trick unravels. We have seconds to spare before the gap closes! Move! NOW!"

The survivors surged to their feet, many of them still chanting. Sweat pouring from their brows, cheeks and everywhere else, they passed through the door and along the flaming road to safety.

■ ■ ■ ■ ■

The air was black, Ellie thought.

Travelling through the forest under the shroud of ash was like tunnelling through soil or ink made solid. She brought up the rear of their ragged column. Missiles of lava still occasionally landed nearby with terrifying, fizzing thuds, and in many places the trees were already aflame. Wildfires chased like ferocious predators through the undergrowth, leaping at their backs. It was only the fact that they were encased in a protective shield generated by Jeremiah's sound waves and Fedir's electromagnetic pulses—as channelled by their new disciples—that preserved them.

The forest vibrated with the low, throaty rumble of so many chanting voices. All the way they were continually harried by the Corrupter's illusions, who jabbed at them with ghastly hallucinations and images of horror, attempting to break the wills of the weaker survivors. Koemi kept their spirits buoyed up with her resounding laughter and ceaseless swells of positive energy.

Still, time seemed to drag on and on in a terrifying, dark loop. It seemed like the torture was going to outlast their stamina as many of the survivors began to stumble. Every time one of them tripped and their chanting fumbled, Ellie's throat clutched in panic. Then, up ahead, something flashed like a diamond, a glittering dart piercing the shadows. This renewed the group's faith, and they put in another spurt of energy. Moments later, the murky curtains of dust parted and the perfect, white outline of a yacht was revealed. The boat gleamed like a beacon, like hope itself.

The small crowd of frightened, soot-scarred and weary survivors erupted out of the smoking forest onto the rough planks of the wharf. A couple of the scientists fell to their knees. There were some cheers, a lot of laughter and tears all around. They were safe, *finally*. Their combined efforts had seen them through the fiery smog of Hell and clean through to the other side. Joy flooded through the party like a sweet fragrance.

But Ellie was distracted.

Underneath the ruckus of her companions' rejoicing, she heard something else, another sound that she didn't understand. A crunching, splintering, smashing noise that was approaching at high speed through the forest behind them. Something—something large and angry—was coming. As the other survivors also heard the commotion, they slowly turned to face the tree line. A number of people took a few nervous steps backwards. It was like a rampaging elephant charging towards them, but they couldn't see it coming.

Finally, the noise arrived and a hulking shape plunged out of the matted perimeter in an explosion of timber shards. It was Venceslao, but a Venceslao nothing like anyone had seen before.

When the Corrupter had directly possessed Logan Vance, his flesh had looked infected, seething like molten metal. On this occasion, Venceslao had inflated to three or four times his original size, into a shuffling, twisted giant. To Ellie, his aura was just as terrifying: a jagged net of thrashing, black spikes that it hurt to look at straight on. He was, quite simply, a monster. The beast's very footprints scalded the wood, and its roar turned Ellie's gut to ice. There were screams and gasps from the other survivors, and a number of them started to sprint towards the boat in terror. The beast pawed the decking, its razor-sharp claws gouging three deep furrows in the wood. It charged!

As the howling fiend barrelled towards the survivors, people dived aside in panic, screaming, pushing and flailing, desperate to escape, driven mad with fear. In the midst of this bedlam, however, at the last moment before the monster struck, Koemi did something amazing.

She stepped out in front of it.

"Koemi, no!" screamed Liza from ten feet away. Sadik, acting automatically, put his arms around the reporter and drew his sidearm to protect her.

Apparently amazed at Koemi's behavior, the beast screeched to a halt mere feet from the slender girl. A few frozen moments slid laboriously past while nothing happened. Clouds of foul steam rose off of Venceslao. Vile, black saliva poured out of its throat and around its teeth, scalding the wooden planks below like boiling tar. The thing could easily have snapped Koemi in two with just one of its deformed paws, yet the diminutive girl didn't flinch. She just stared mildly up into its foul face with a faint smile curving her lips.

Then she started to laugh.

Despite its lethal appearance, she just giggled at the demon exactly as if it were a kitten playing in the grass. It was the most bizarre thing in the world. It was the act of a crazy person. *A suicide bid,* thought Ellie for an instant. Then she saw the effect Koemi's laughter had on the beast and she understood.

Venceslao flinched.

It was just the tiniest of minute twitches; surely everyone else was far too agitated to have caught it, but that twitch told Ellie all she needed to know. She moved next to Koemi and began to laugh at the creature.

"What are you doing?" demanded Kauser hotly, waving his pistol. "Step aside. Let me get a clear shot!"

"No, Sadik, no violence," called Koemi in her bell-like tone. "We do not need it to defeat this miserable creature."

"I'll shoot it!" Kauser yelled hoarsely. "It'll kill us all—"

"No, laughter is enough," said Jeremiah as he moved to join the others. "This is the Corrupter's last secret, its crucial weakness."

Ellie took up the explanation next.

"It has no power over those who do not fear, you see," she told them all. "And no one here in this group has any fear left. We've come through all that this thing can throw at us, and we survived. If we work together there is nothing humans cannot achieve. So, join us now. Let us laugh in the face of evil!"

Slowly, they did. A few nervous guffaws at first, then a steady trickle of giggles.

"No, your flesh will burn! I will devour your souls! I have dark powers beyond your imagination!" hissed the Venceslao creature in a sizzling, gurgling voice, but the effect was more comical than terrifying and it simply caused more of the scientists to laugh.

The trickles soon became a stream that became a *torrent,* and swiftly the whole dock was filled with hysterics. In the midst of that irrepressible gale of giggles, Ellie thought she heard the harsh yet strangely melodic echo of an old man's laughter, but she couldn't be sure.

The Corrupter in Venceslao cowered back, retreating as if from an unbearable heat. No! It wasn't merely retreating…it was actually *shrinking*, dwindling away as it atrophied back down towards Venceslao's original size! The beast deflated, its horror dissipating until only the shrivelled body of Venceslao remained. He dropped to the wooden slats of the jetty like an empty sack and lay there breathing weakly, his eyes empty. Only the Healers heard the distant, thin screech of the Corrupter fading away, fading to nothing. Koemi walked over to Venceslao and stood over him.

"I forgive you," she said quietly. All the other Healers joined her and repeated those words. Liza Brooks was aghast.

"But you can't, not after everything he's done."

"We must. We can't pick and choose who gets offered our gifts and who doesn't," said Ellie.

"If we did that, then we'd be just the same as him," Harata added solemnly.

"We'll heal him, too, in the hope that he recovers and—with time—perhaps finally sheds his hatred and fear."

They saw in the tilt of Liza's chin that she understood and offered her approval. So then it was truly over. They had won. A great joy settled among the group as they got ready to leave the island for good. Venceslao's ex-soldiers and scientists all turned to each other and laughed in happy release. Grinning, everyone quickly pitched in to prepare the yacht for departure. The vessel's original crew were overseeing the task and it was hard work, but the faces were smiling in spite of the continued darkness overhead. While people dashed around Liza, she grabbed the arm of a dazed-looking researcher and shook him until he looked at her directly.

"Hey, can your laptop work with that satellite phone?"

"Ah, I guess," the researcher stammered.

"Could I upload something, video footage from a cell phone?"

"Don't see why not. Who to?"

"My former editor. I once promised him the story of the millennium, and now I'm finally going to deliver!"

While the researcher occupied himself with booting up his computer, Liza's gaze wandered over to Sadik Kauser. Their eyes met, and they shared a moment. The captain broke the contact. Uncharacteristically awkward, Liza smiled wryly to herself, then set about uploading her footage of their escape and the Healers' powers, as well as how they taught them to all the survivors.

"Give this to all the TV stations, all the internet sites, everyone. This is the biggest story you'll EVER break," she wrote in an e-mail to Evan Getz before signing off for good with an airy sigh.

Then she walked directly over to Captain Sadik Kauser, formerly of Pakistan's Inter-Services Intelligence Agency, and firmly took his hand. The quiet, reserved man blinked at her in surprise, which made her chuckle inside, but then he squeezed her palm gently in return. His skin was warm and surprisingly soft.

They watched the crew unfurl the sails together. Soon they would be going home.

Fifteen minutes later, all the survivors were onboard, and Faraja, Koemi, Harata, Jorge, Fedir, Jeremiah and Ellie all trooped along the gangplank. Liza Brooks followed next, and Sadik Kauser was the last to leave.

He stood for a moment, staring back into the black inferno at the heart of the island, smartly saluted once, then stepped off the dock for the last time.

◼ ◼ ◼ ◼ ◼

Black ash continued to clog up the sky in roiling eddies, but as the ship forged out to sea, it seemed like they might be emerging from the worst of it. Flakes of gray, cancerous snow still smeared themselves onto the cockpit windows, but it did seem to Ellie that the acrid tendrils that curled around the hull might have been thinning slightly. She walked to the bow of the ship and stood, with her hands against the cool, metal railing, staring out into the darkness. She squinted. *Was that a pale patch way off in the distance, or just a trick of her imagination?*

After a moment, little Koemi joined her, grinning. Koemi's smile was so infectious that Ellie couldn't *not* respond, and when she did, she automatically felt that everything was going to be all right. Tough, plucky Harata arrived next. She didn't smile exactly but tipped up her proud chin and threw her clear gaze ahead. Down below on the railing, her fingers took hold of Ellie's and Koemi's hands, linking the three of them.

"You could use your far-sight to see what is out there before the rest of us," Ellie told Harata quietly.

"I know," her friend answered after a moment's hesitation. "But we need to face whatever comes next together."

Ellie nodded in understanding. They were bonded now, their destinies braided into one single purpose. They were born to heal the world. Gradually the other Healers gathered silently at the bow: friendly busybody Faraja, eager Jorge, thoughtful Fedir and gentle, sweet Jeremiah. They all joined hands. Liza's story was already beaming out around the world, and news of their existence would soon be known to millions. Hopefully, their message would echo in the heart of everyone who heard it, but nothing was guaranteed. The only thing that was certain was that their lives would never be the same again.

Now Ellie could definitely see a soft glow filtering through the darkness ahead. Seven sets of eyes focused on its pearly promise. Leaning on the railing, the Healers waited, unafraid and hopeful, as they headed into the light. The sky overhead was finally clearing, and it was time for the next stage of their journey to begin.

For more information visit www.myidentifiers.com

23528121R00155

Made in the USA
Charleston, SC
25 October 2013